"While reading *Sand Tarts, Pies, and Devils in Disguise*, you'll feel like you're relaxing on the front porch in a wicker rocker with a tall glass of sweet tea catching up with an old friend—or several old friends, as the case may be. Save a chair for me!"

—Gayle Trent, author of *Killer Sweet Tooth*

Sand Tarts, Pies, and Devils in Disguise

Lisa Hall

Mountain Girl Press
Bristol, Virginia

This is a work of fiction. Any resemblance to actual persons, either living or dead is entirely coincidental. All names, characters, and events are the product of the author's imagination.

Sand Tarts, Pies, and Devils in Disguise

Mountain Girl Press
Published November 2011

Cover art by Pam Keaton
www.pamkeaton.com

You may contact the publisher at:
Mountain Girl Press
2195 Euclid Avenue, Suite 7
Bristol, VA 24201
E-mail: publisher@mountaingirlpress.com

ISBN: 978-0-9846398-9-2
PCN: 2011939618

The Cutie Pies Chronicles

This book is dedicated to my husband Todd.
Thank you for supporting my dreams and
filling my life wih love!

Chapter 1

"Responsible, mature women do not flippantly leave their families just so they can go trotting off to the ocean for a week with their girlfriends. Sounds like those three are in a hurry to high-tail it out of town so they can get W-I-L-D." Dorothy just overheard her office-mate Patsy talking on the phone. She could not believe the vile things Patsy was saying about her upcoming trip to Hilton Head.

Dorothy pinned some hope on the belief Patsy completely changed her ways. In recent months, Patsy was nice enough to make Dorothy feel bad for ever thinking that she was a horrible person. After hearing Patsy talk on the phone, Dorothy was wondering if the saying "A tiger never changes his stripes" was true. Patsy sure was sounding a lot like she did in the old days.

As soon as it came time to take her lunch break, Dorothy went out to her car and called Marlene on her cell phone to relay what was said.

"Marlene, Patsy was talking in her cubicle. She did not realize I was hearing every word she said. I'd been in a meeting all morning, and she did not know I came back. That woman was talking dreadful crap about all of us. She said taking off for the beach was something a bunch of teenage girls would do. It took everything in me not to grab that phone out of her hand

and beat her over the head with it till she's senseless. Well, she's already senseless. I don't think she's ever had much sense, but you know what I mean."

"Dorothy, I'm with you. I've had many a violent thought when it comes to Patsy and her pals. You don't know how many times I've prayed for God to grant me the patience and strength to deal with those women," said Marlene.

Marlene could only imagine what Patsy McCrumb and friends had spouted off in recent days. Patsy and her pals had been lying pretty low for months, but there seemed to be a resurrection occurring. Though they might never reach the potency of times past, Marlene could sense Patsy and friends were getting back to some of their old tricks. Marlene and most others in the town of Coleman hated to see it coming. The town rejoiced in a period of respite from drama and controversy. Patsy and her friends had been part of the Coleman Canasta Club, and were also known as the Hens to the rest of the town. For decades, the Hens' mean-spirited gossip and meddling caused problems in an otherwise idyllic little Southwest Virginia town.

Their craft was gossip, and the Hens had became masters. They worked with lies and baseless assumptions and pieced them together like an intricate quilt. Mere scraps of truth foraged from here, there and everywhere were stitched together to create elaborate and epic tales.

For many years, the Hens were a tight-knit group, bound by their adoration of back-fence talk. Eventually, the bad deeds so deeply seeped into their souls they turned on each other. Deception and dishonesty was fine until those in their own circle were deceived and lied to. The kind of poison that spewed from their mouths for years proved deadly when they used it on each other. The gossip and backstabbing that kept the club alive and kicking for so many years, was the cause of its ultimate demise. The town's people of Coleman hoped the Hens had seen the light of day and learned their lesson.

2

In the aftermath of the club breaking up, many Hens appeared to have retreated from the evil that permeated their lives. Some sought atonement by carrying out some very good deeds. Before long, the Hens were on a path to redemption, getting back into the good graces of everyone they previously offended.

Dorothy was a primary beneficiary of those good deeds. She was diagnosed with breast cancer right around the time the Hens parted ways. Patsy and several of her friends really stepped up to help Dorothy. The boundless generosity and compassion they showed was something Dorothy never thought any of them were capable of.

Patsy covered for her at work so Dorothy would not get behind or have to sacrifice pay on her days off. Several of the Hens showed up at Dorothy's front door on a regular basis with meals, fresh flowers and little books and toys for Dorothy's daughter. Dorothy was at first apprehensive and skeptical about trusting the Hens to do nice things without ulterior motives. However, after it was all said and done, she honestly did not know how she could have gotten through her treatments without Patsy and other Hens pitching in to help.

Over weeks and months, the good deeds began to diminish and the new version of old Hens was beginning to hatch. They did not slip completely back into their old ways. Their stance softened considerably, but they had not entirely retreated from slamming down other people with their negative talk and innuendos. What before might have been a verbal punch in the nose was delivered as more of a little tap on the shoulder. It was a, "Hey, we're not going to talk too badly about you, and we won't make up blatant lies, but we will still discuss your business, repeat things without having our facts straight, feel like we know how to run your life better than you do and weigh in with our poorly informed opinions."

The women were organized under a new name and purpose. They went from canasta to casseroles. The Coleman Canasta Club had been revamped as the Coleman Supper Club.

Every month, they met at a member's house to enjoy carefully prepared food and ill-created rumors. The dining and dishing would last for hours. Supper Club members left meetings will their bellies full of food and their minds clogged with dirty details on other folks in town.

In its final years, the Coleman Canasta Club never really bothered to play the game of canasta. The entire purpose of the club was having a reason to gather together and gossip. The Coleman Supper Club would eventually dishonor its name and mission too. In the beginning, the hostess for the evening's meeting would prepare a four-course feast for their meeting. The meetings began with appetizers, followed by salads, the main meal and then dessert. Soon, the appetizers and salads were dropped from the menu. The last meeting's dinner consisted of take-out pizza and ice cream sandwiches. The Coleman Supper Club was increasingly becoming less about the suppers and more about tasty tidbits of titillating talk.

From what Dorothy had overheard from Patsy's conversation, the fact that she, Marlene and Allison were taking off on a girls only trip was the final course of the last supper club meeting. Apparently their appetites for gossip were not satisfied that night, for Patsy and crew were still chomping.

Because of the kindness showed during her illness, Dorothy found it impossible to dislike the Hens with the same vim and vigor as before. Like most people, the Hens were two-sided coins. They had an evil side, and they had a good side. It was always a toss-up as to which side you were going to see. Because Dorothy knew how lovely that good side could be, she overlooked many things that happened when the bad side was facing up.

Dorothy and Patsy's relationship was now at a place where Dorothy could throw it right back at her when Patsy got a little out of line. Dorothy thought about letting Patsy know she overheard the bad things that were said. The comments Patsy made that day bothered Dorothy, but she was going to let it slide. The

4

condo they were going to be staying in belonged to Patsy and her husband. The trip was so needed and well-deserved that Dorothy would not have dared taken the risk of Patsy and Larry reneging on their offer.

Patsy's husband, Larry, owned the accounting office where both Dorothy and Patsy were employed. Larry had promised Dorothy their condo in Hilton Head for the week. With their vacation at stake, Dorothy thought venting to her friend would be a much safer option than confronting Patsy. It was a gutless but wise decision that was made to protect their plans to spend a precious week together with no husbands or kids.

Dorothy, Marlene and Allison were using the week for a girls vacation they all needed in the worst way. Dorothy's recent bout with breast cancer and the combat-related death of Allison's brother-in-law had strengthened their bonds of friendship strong beyond measure. Marlene's life had not been so wrought with struggles in recent years, but balancing a successful business and motherhood always made her a good candidate for a vacation.

They were looking forward to an entire week of fun and relaxation in an oceanfront condo. The girls anticipated their days beginning with a nice walk followed by a pot of coffee and breakfast on the screened-in porch. The rest of the day's schedule would include hanging out on the beach, a quick lunch,then more time on the beach. In the late afternoons, they would come in, have a round of Diet Cokes and a short nap. After cleaning up and getting into pretty sundresses and sandals, the ladies would go to dinner, come back to the condo for an evening walk on the beach, some wine, chick flicks and late night talks.

That was their basic plan, but it allowed for some flexibility. Each lady had something on their agenda they hoped to build into the schedule. Marlene wanted to take a day trip to Savannah. Dorothy wanted to see the lighthouse at Harbour Town, and Allison had promised her kids she would buy them T-shirts from the Salty Dog.

Dorothy could not bring herself to call Patsy out, but she sure could rant to Marlene.

"The first thing she said is that I ought to be taking my family on this trip. Originally, I had thought about taking Tom and Darla, but Tom has been booked for six months to photograph a wedding in Langrid, so there's no way he could go out of town. To be honest, I'm glad it's a girls trip. We do a family vacation every year. I've been longing to do a trip with my friends for years. Family vacations are great, but chasing Darla around the beach for seven days is not exactly restful. The Hens also worry that I have not been in remission long enough to travel. Patsy says she thinks I'll have a set-back in my recovery from going on this trip. Sometimes, it seems like Patsy and her friends think I ought to just retire to my bed for the rest of my life, for fear that I might get sick again."

Marlene was sure Patsy and her friends had something to say about her leaving town, also. They had analyzed and scrutinized nearly every move Marlene made for most of her life. "Okay Dorothy, lay it on me. What did they say about me?"

"Oh, they can't believe that you are abandoning your business for a week when the new Walmart is practically breathing its hot breath down your neck and knocking at your back door like the big, bad wolf. They've barely broken ground, but Patsy was talking like that Walmart's going to be constructed, opened and putting you out of business within the week's time that we're gone."

If Marlene was half as worried about Walmart coming to town as Patsy and friends thought she should be, there would already be a "For Sale" sign on her door. "They think the big bad wolf is coming to town to destroy my business" she said. "They don't know that I don't give up easily. I'm really not that worried. Alright Dorothy, I know they didn't just talk about my business. What else did the have to say?"

"Of course they had to say something about you leaving your hot 'Cubano' alone for a week. They think he may stray because it's in his blood."

Mark, Marlene's husband, was one quarter Cuban, or "Cubano" as the Hens referred to him. The Hens' notions of Latino men were all based on Desi Arnaz. Since Desi cheated on Lucille Ball, they assumed that Mark would also cheat on Marlene.

Dorothy continued, "They also bet that you will be wearing some itty-bitty bikini. Patsy said you're too old to wear a two-piece."

At forty-five, Marlene had no problem rocking a two-piece. The Hens predicted that pregnancy would wreck Marlene's figure. Good genes and regular workouts had her back in swimsuit shape within months of giving birth.

Motherhood had in no way tempted Marlene to let her weight get out of hand or to let go of her sense of style. With her tousled auburn hair, big green eyes and a whimsical sprinkling freckles across her nose, Marlene had a look that was a perfect combination of glamorous yet effortless.

"Now, what have they said about Allison?" asked Marlene.

Dorothy began, "Among the more trivial matters, they think her ponytail is too long. Patsy thinks Allison is still trying to look like a high school cheerleader."

Allison had worn her hair at shoulder length for quite some time. Over the past year she had grown it out a few more inches, just for a change. The Hens thought a lady over forty should not be wearing her hair that long, unless it was pinned up in a bun.

The long blond hair, usually pulled into a low ponytail, looked just fine on Allison. She was petite with bright blue eyes and a smile that could light up a room. Allison liked wearing her hair in a ponytail because it was a simple way for a busy mom of two active kids to get out the door every morning. If being cute made a grown woman look like a high school cheerleader, Allison was doomed to look like a cheerleader for life.

Dorothy went on to tell some of the more hurtful things the Hens said about Allison.

"They cannot understand how Allison can leave Gary in his time of grief. It has been surmised that Allison is thinking about leaving him for good. Patsy said she would not be surprised if Allison met some man at the beach and never came back to Gary."

Marlene had talked to Allison earlier that day. Allison was struggling with whether or not to go on the trip. "Dorothy, Allison has stressed so much over taking this trip. She has decided after much thought that she needs to get a break from the sadness and heaviness in her house. It's all starting to really bring her down."

Allison being brought down was an unusual event. She was the type to bring sunshine to a cloudy day with her sassy, perky persona. Trying to help Gary out of his depression had Allison at her wits end.

"Tonight she said that she doesn't think he even notices whether or not she's around anyway" said Marlene. She thinks leaving might be good for him. What bothers Allison most is his withdrawing from the normal family stuff that he always took part in before. Leaving town will force him to resume some of his activities with the kids. Gary hasn't been to even one of their ballgames since Mitch died."

Dorothy planned to call Allison that evening. "I will try and be reassuring when I talk to Allison later. She needs this for herself. Allison has to realize that Mitch is grieving in his own way, at his own pace. She can't do anything to help him along if he has decided to withdraw. The only way for her to decompress a little is to get away from home. If she can't keep her own spirits up, she sure won't be of any help to him or their kids."

Dorothy had to make sure of one last thing before she hung up. "Marlene, I know I've been asking you everyday for a week, but are you packed yet?"

Marlene's mind was wildly creative but not particularly organized. Since kindergarten, Dorothy had taken it upon herself to go behind Marlene to make sure that life's most miniscule details were never overlooked. It was Dorothy who, on their very first day of elementary school, kept reminding Marlene to not talk in class, walk single file down the hallway and put her crayons back in the box. Forty years later, Dorothy was still making sure that her best friend packed sunscreen and flip flops for their beach trip.

Dorothy kept running down a checklist, making sure Marlene had everything she needed for the trip. As always, Dorothy was focused on the little nit-picky details that Marlene saw as no big deal. "Hey Dorothy, don't worry about it. It's not like we're headed to Outer Mongolia. There's a Target about two miles from our condo. If I forget something, I'm sure I can purchase it in Hilton Head. There are a heck of a lot more places to shop there than in Coleman. Besides, I'm sure you'll have your stash of looted hotel items in case we forget anything."

Marlene was referring the enormous stockpile of shampoo, soap and other items Dorothy collected from hotel stays over the years. No toiletry or mini-sewing kit had ever been left behind in a hotel room by Dorothy. She never took a towel or washcloth. Those were off-limits, but everything on the bathroom counter was hers to take home. The little coffee packs and sweeteners were also nabbed by Dorothy, as well as the hotel stationary and ink pens.

Dorothy's family had a way of thinking that had carried over from the Great Depression. They practiced a form of organized hoarding. It gave them a tremendous sense of comfort to think if they were to fall upon hard times, they would at least have some travel sized toiletries and little notepads with hotel emblems.

"You'll be thankful for my stash if you forget your shampoo" said Dorothy.

"Dorothy, every tourist in Hilton Head could forget their shampoo" said Marlene. Your stash would be enough to cover everyone. If there is ever a natural disaster, and I cannot get any shampoo or conditioner, I'm coming to your house."

Dorothy was sufficiently satisfied Marlene was indeed ready for their trip. "Okay, I'll give you a break. Now, it's on to Allison. I'll check and make sure that she has everything in order. I can't wait until we get there!"

Dorothy was afraid she might be getting on Marlene and Allison's nerves with her incessant need to take care of everyone. She knew her friends were quite competent to prepare for their trip on their own. However, after so many months of other people having to take care of her during her cancer treatments, it felt so good to be the one watching out for others. Not that Dorothy did not appreciate all of the casseroles delivered to her house, free babysitting, cards, flowers and prayers. All of that meant a great deal to her. It has just been strangely uncomfortable for Dorothy to accept help from others. Now that she was no longer taking cancer treatments, Dorothy was happy to be back in the role of taking care of everyone else. She was at a lost to find ways to help her friends as much as they had helped her. A simple "thank you" felt embarrassingly insufficient. Her only hope was that she had not become overzealous in her efforts. The last thing she wanted to be was overbearing.

Dorothy made a little pact with herself. "I will not be too controlling, mothering or otherwise overbearing with my friends, lest I completely drive them nuts on our trip!"

* * *

Later that evening, Dorothy called Allison. The trip could not come soon enough for her. "Dorothy, I'm packed and I've gone over check-list time and time again", said Allison. I'm so excited that I'm going to have to take a Tylenol PM so that I can go to sleep tonight. I'd take off right this minute if I could. That sounds terrible to say, but I need to get away from here so badly. I know I'll miss the kids and Gary, but I've been drug down so far by Gary's emotional rut that I feel like I'm trying to swim the English Channel with an anchor tied around my waist. It's just exhausting!"

The girls trip was going to be a form of self preservation for Allison. Although she often felt like she might lose it, that was not an option. It was up to her to hold things together. A week was going to make coping with her situation much easier.

Allison's husband Gary and both of his parents spent most of their time in another zone ever since Mitch's death. It was not as if Allison expected any of them to get over Mitch's passing. That would never happen. The grief would forever be an undercurrent in their lives. It would always be there to pull them under at certain times. Allison's only expectation had been that things might greatly improve with time.

That's what she got for having expectations about other people's grief. Making predictions and prescriptions for how long and how hard they needed to grieve Mitch's death was more ludicrous than trying to pinpoint the end of time.

Soon after Mitch died, it seemed that Gary and his parents had found solace and purpose in collecting items for soldiers' care packages. They later named the project "Love, Mitch." At first, the project was a positive thing that gave them an outlet for their grief. It was what Allison thought would help heal Gary's hurt.

Allison was beginning to wonder if throwing themselves headlong into that task had short-circuited their grieving process. Mitch and his parents had become so obsessed with the project that they were ignoring most other aspects of their lives. Collecting items for care packages had so filled their days that Mitch's family barely had time to breathe, much less mourn. When he was not filling care packages, Gary was so tired that he spent time in the basement all by himself.

There were very few times when Allison had seen Gary cry since Mitch's death. It seemed like he always did a little better after a good cry. Allison thought of his grief like a water blister.

Crying was like draining the blister. Draining it would not keep it from coming back, but it made things feel better for a time. She would love to have seen Gary and his parents letting things out with an occasional good cry, but instead they obsessed over the care packages.

As far as other parts of their lives, forget it. They were going through the motions; showing up for work and attending some family functions. Physical presence was the extent of it. Emotional vacancy was usually all any of them could offer. Allison often thought that cardboard stand-ins would be more fun to be around than Gary and his parents.

There were brief and beautiful moments when Allison saw the old Gary come back. She held onto those moments like photos in a scrapbook, flipping back to them in her mind. Allison hoped that those moments would become more frequent as time moved on. Instead, it seemed that every day chipped away a little more of Gary's spirit. Allison wondered what, if any, would remain of the man she once knew. He was like a stranger. There was no sparkle left in his eyes, which were usually downcast. When Gary talked, his voice was a quiet monotone, and his speech pattern was so slow that listening to him made Allison want to yawn. Talking to him had become difficult and awkward. Conversation was something Gary did not seem to want. What irked Allison the most was when she or the kids would try and talk to him at home, and he would stare at the television, or refuse to look up from reading a book or newspaper. He had gotten good at using the television, or whatever he was reading, as a barrier to shield him from having to connect with his family. Gary seemed terrified and uncomfortable if she or the kids looked directly at him. His eyes would dart wildly in another direction, as if he were protecting himself or them from what was going on behind his eyes.

It had come to a point where Allison was getting almost nothing from her marriage. She felt so supremely selfish when she admitted to herself, and nobody else, that she sometimes wondered how much longer she could take it. She and Gary shared a home, but that and their children had become their only connection. "Dorothy, I hope this trip forces Gary to think about what life might be like without me around to take care of things while he's MIA" said Allison. "He's going to be working, plus taking care of the kids, the house, the fish and the dog all by himself. I know he's this way because he lost his brother. He needs to realize how much worse things could be if he lost me too."

Dorothy had not heard Allison say anything so unkind about Gary since way back in college when he briefly broke her heart. Gary had been in love with Allison since they were kids. Allison was his one and only. She could not imagine Gary without Allison. They had always been like two pieces of the same puzzle; quite different, but made to perfectly fit together. Gary was the tall, dark and handsome counterpart to his petite, blond wife. "Honey, you're not thinking about leaving Gary, are you?"

Chapter 2

Monique relished going to the mailbox. That unopened stack of mail was something she always saw as a bundle of exciting possibilities. There might be a new magazine she could look forward to reading that evening or a postcard from some faraway place from her brother's travels. Lately, Monique had been getting envelopes stuffed with photographs of babies. Most of her friends and cousins had started their families, and Monique and Bo hoped that they would soon be doing the same.

After work each day, Monique's ritual was to check the answering machine then walk out to the mailbox. That evening, in her mailbox was a padded manila envelope. *Oh goody*, she thought. *Must be something good!*

A closer look the box revealed there was not a return address. The postmark was from Beckley, West Virginia. When Monique got something from Beckley, she never knew whether to be happy or nervous. She left behind a sordid past in a West Virginia strip bar. Lots of friends from that past turned their lives in a more positive direction, just as Monique had done. She thought the envelope was probably from one of those old friends. At least, she hoped it was from one of them.

There were also some really bad people who had come into her life while she was in Beckley. Monique often worried that one of those people would pop back into her life. It was a nagging paranoia that sometimes hung over Monique like a swarm of wasps. She always had to wonder if one of those wasps would buzz down to Coleman to sting her!

When Monique got back into the house, she opened the padded envelope first. Inside there was no note; just a DVD in inside a plastic case. Neither the DVD nor the case was labeled. Monique did not know whether to watch the DVD or go outside and toss it like a Frisbee into the woods behind her house.

Monique knew for a fact there were some videos of her she would prefer did not exist. When she worked as an exotic dancer, she took a few jobs dancing at bachelor parties for extra money. Most grooms-to-be were not keen on having video or photographic evidence of their wild night before nuptials floating around, just waiting to fall in the hands of their beloved. There were those few who were willing to tempt fate by setting up video cameras in the corner or having their buddies take a few raunchy photographs. Monique stopped dancing before everyone had video on their mobile phones, but there still were enough pictures and videos to make her nervous.

The more she looked at the mysterious DVD, the more she feared what its contents might be. If it were of her stripping or doing some other act from her past, she could not stand the thought of seeing even one second of footage. Monique popped the DVD out of its case, and stared as if it would reveal itself to her.

She felt of sense of urgency to do something about the DVD. When she looked at the clock, she realized that Bo would be coming home within an hour or so. What bothered her most was she did not want to tell Bo about the mysterious package. Usually if Monique were troubled by something, the first thing she would want to do would be tell Bo. He knew everything about Monique and her past, and he never judged his wife. When one well-meaning aunt asked Bo, "Aren't you concerned that Monique may miss her old life? What if she still has a wild hair?" Bo reminded his aunt of what happened with his cousin Ronald.

"Everyone thought Ronald's wife Lou was the perfect, most innocent creature in the universe until she decided she needed to catch up on all the wild times she missed. Monique did some things she regrets, but at least she's sewn her wild oats. It's out of her system. She's ready to settle down."

Bo's cousin Ronald married a young lady named Lou who appeared to be pure as the driven snow. Lou never dated anybody but Ronald. She never ever smoked a cigarette, tasted beer or uttered a curse word. After seven years of marriage and two babies, Lou went crazy and decided to take a little walk on the wild side. That little walk took her whole life on a crazy, twisted detour.

Lou started going to honky-tonks and got her belly-button pierced and started wearing tops that barely covered her boobs. She definitely did not cover that pierced belly button. Ronald convinced himself that his wife was just hitting her wild phase a little late in life.

He had seen a show about the Amish. The Amish let their kids take some time away from being Amish so they can see if they really want to follow the strict religions for the rest of their life. Some of them go buck-wild and then wind up back in a bonnet and being Amish again.

His hope was that she would soon get tired of her late nights of carousing and come back to him and the kids. Ronald wanted Lou to miss her old life. Instead, Lou left him and their kids for a guy she met in a bar.

Bo had always taken up for Monique with anyone who questioned why he chose her when he could have his pick of women. He was willing to leave her past in the past. To him, it was dead and buried. Monique had to wonder how understanding her husband would be if someone had dug something back up.

When Monique was young, they had a little beagle named Jinx that just loved to hunt. That dog used to kill any vermin that came within ten yards of him. No squirrel, rabbit, chipmunk or ground hog was safe when Jinx was around.

Jinx had a bad habit of littering their yard with the carcasses from his kills. Monique's dad would bury the remains down in the woods behind their house, and Jinx would always track the scent and dig them back up.

Many of the men from Monique's past were more like dogs than human beings. A good number of them would be capable of digging up what she thought was dead and buried and throwing it right in her front yard.

A mental picture went though Monique's mind of her dad carrying his shovel down into the woods to bury Jinx's victims. Bo kept a shovel in their garage, there were woods behind their house and he would be getting home from the farm in about 45 minutes.

Chapter 3

Emily and Anna Patton did not date very much. They had a sum total of five dates between them. They were about to add a date to that total, or maybe two dates, depending on how things were looked at.

The twins were getting ready to go on a double date with the Butler brothers. The Butlers were not twins but brothers born two years apart. The Patton girls met the Butler brothers when their family presented a musical performance at Carson-Newman College in Jefferson City, Tennessee.

Emily and Anna were quite accomplished as musicians. Both could sing like angels straight out of Heaven. Their talents were not limited to vocals. Each knew how to play just about anything on the piano. Emily could also play the fiddle and dulcimer. Anna played the guitar and banjo.

Musicality was a family tradition. For generations, their family spent many evenings practicing their craft. Southern gospel was their preferred musical genre. With their television viewing limited to mostly news programs and G rated movies, music was the family's form of nightly entertainment.

The family sometimes shared the gift of their talents by taking their act outside of the home. They played for the congregation at their church for years. Recently the family began playing in other churches and in local festivals.

They called themselves the Patton Family Glory Band. The band consisted of Emily, Anna, their sister, two brothers and their parents. It was difficult for their pastor to convince them to take their show outside the walls of their own church.

The Pattons were humble people to the point of being almost bashful. It took their longtime and trusted pastor to convince them that they were not being proud or pompous if they began playing their music to a wider audience.

"It is not a sin to have confidence in the gift that God has bestowed upon you," said the pastor. Sharing that talent is sharing God's blessing. In turn, your music will bless other people. Preaching is how I share the gospel. Music is how your family can share the gospel."

After some prayerful contemplation, Emily and Ann's father decided that it would be acceptable to sing at other churches and some local events. They were doing it for the glory of the Lord, but Emily and Anna's mother and daddy also prayed that it might be a means for their girls to meet nice, single young Christian boys who were looking for sweet, old-fashioned young ladies.

The Pattons kept their children out of the mainstream culture. All of the kids were homeschooled. Other than participating in community sports leagues and scouts, the Patton kids were rarely around kids outside of their own family and church.

While their parents had no regrets about the way they had raised their kids, they knew their somewhat isolated lifestyle might make it hard for their children to find mates. Their daddy feared that Emily and Anna might have a future like their cousins, Ruth and Ruby.

Ruth and Ruby were the twin daughters of Emily and Anna's Aunt Estelle and Uncle Claude.

Identical twins ran on both sides of the Patton family. Since Estelle was the sister of Emily and Anna's mom, and Claude was the brother of Emily and Anna's dad, Ruth and Ruby were double-first cousins.

Ruth and Ruby were five years older than Emily and Anna. Their family raised them in a similar fashion by homeschooling and carefully monitoring outside influences. Ruth and Ruby's world became such a safe cocoon that the world outside their home and church had become a frightening place.

Neither Ruth nor Ruby had jobs. If they went out to eat or did anything social, it was only with each other. Ruth and Ruby were two cute young adult ladies who lived as if they were old spinsters. They reminded some folk of the Baldwin sisters from *The Waltons*, except their lives were not nearly so dramatic.

Emily and Anna's parents did not want that lonely, stagnant life for their daughters. Their hope was that Emily and Anna might marry and have families of their own. They prayed their daughters might have a way to meet nice church boys. Perhaps getting to perform their gospel music could provide an answer to the Patton parents' prayers.

Emily and Anna certainly got the attention of some church boys. A pastor at one church joked that "Our young male demographic jumps dramatically when The Patton Family Glory Band visits our church."

Some young lads who only came to church on Easter Sunday would drag themselves out of bed, put on their Sunday best, and come to church just to sit in the sanctuary to get a glimpse of Emily and Anna. The twins, with their pretty little faces, and perfect little figures, had some boys thinking unholy thoughts. They were a strange combination of Holly Hobby meets Pam Anderson, which made them utterly enticing to the opposite sex.

It would take a couple of exceptional boys to win the hearts of the Patton twins. Emily and Anna were as pure and holy as the hymns they sang. Their standards were loftier than most boys their age could ever attain. Emily and Anna desired men of God; spiritual men who did not drink, smoke or otherwise purvey in carnal pleasure. Those qualities were quite hard to find amongst young twenty-somethings. Still, if they were to find that type of man, they were most likely to do it in a church or other place where people were gathered to hear gospel music.

The Butler boys, it seemed, might be the young men who would finally rise to the high standards of Emily and Anna. They had not been quite as sheltered as Emily and Anna, but their parents still kept them away from many worldly temptations.

The boys had gone to Christian schools all their lives. When it came time for college, they decided on Carson-Newman College. Attending the small Baptist college nestled in the hills of Tennessee was a Butler family tradition. Their mother and father had met while students at Carson-Newman.

Brad and Brent had impressive resumes in and out of the classroom. Brad was a junior majoring in education. He had dark brown wavy hair, blue-green eyes and a tall, thin frame. Brent was a freshman majoring in religion. He was a couple of inches shorter than his brother. Brent had blond wavy hair, but the same color of eyes as his brother. In their courses, they both pulled off nearly perfect GPAs. Off-campus, Brad coached a little league team, and Brent worked with a youth group from a local church. They were seemingly exemplary males who had some ideas about how to score points with a father. They were sure to be extra respectful when the spoke to Emily and Anna's dad about having an event following the Patton Family Glory Band's performance at the college.

The Patton Family Glory Band had been invited to play for a community life and worship program at Carson-Newman. Students of the college were required to attend ten of the programs per semester. The services were a way of supplementing the Christian curriculum by promoting faith and a sense of community on the campus. Carson-Newman went to great lengths to offer a variety of programs for their students to choose from. Traditional sermons, interpretive dance, dramatic productions,

Christian humorists and musical performances were among the choices.

As soon as the posters went up promoting The Patton's appearance, male students began making plans to attend. Although they were mostly not into technology, the Patton's cousin did make a video snippet of the family performing to put on YouTube. Watching that video became the guilty pleasure of several young Carson-Newman males.

As if there were not enough fanfare surrounding the Patton's appearance on campus,the student government association planned a cupcake and sparkling punch reception following the performance. Brad and Brent were the original force behind the cake and punch plan.

Both boys were elected to the Student Government Association. Upon becoming obsessed with watching the Patton video that was put on YouTube, they decided they had to find a way to meet Emily and Anna.

Brad and Brent knew that with it being an evening service, the family was likely to leave immediately following their performance. A reception held in their honor was a sure way to keep them on campus a little longer.

Brad approached the head of the home economics department with an idea. "Would one of your classes be willing to do a cake and punch reception following Monday night's program in the chapel" he asked?

The home ec department was always looking for events to host so their students could gain experience in event-planning/catering. A group of ladies in one of the courses chose to go with something fun and whimsical.

They had seen a feature in *Southern Living* on a mini-cupcake and sparkling wine party. They decided to go with the theme, changing the sparkling wine to a sparkling punch.

Brad and Brent took turns calling the Patton's house to relay details of the reception. Mr. Patton answered the phone each time, and both boys were extra prudent in trying to make a good impression on the father of the young ladies they hoped to court.

The Patton's performance was held in the sanctuary of the First Baptist Church, located on Carson-Newman's campus. After the Pattons sang, everyone made their way downstairs to the church fellowship hall, where the cupcake and sparkling punch reception was set up.

The home economics ladies did a fabulous job with the reception. Lavender and silver balloons were all over the fellowship hall. Tiered cake stands held mini-cupcakes in several flavors. Half of the cupcakes were basic vanilla, chocolate and coconut. The others were spring-inspired fruity flavors like pink lemonade, white-chocolate raspberry, strawberry shortcake, orange, lemon and key lime. On the drink table, silver punch bowls held a bubbly mixture of white grape juice and ginger ale.

Lots of students lined up to meet the Pattons during the reception. Brad and Brent were on call for cupcake and punch duty. They took on the responsibility of making sure the family had plenty of cupcakes and punch to snack on while they met their fans.

After the reception, they helped the Pattons load all of their equipment in their van for the ride home. It was during the walk to the van that Brad got the nerve to ask Emily and Anna to go out with him and his brother.

"Girls, my brother and I would love it if we could drive up to Coleman and take you two out to dinner," he said.

Emily and Anna both turned red as beets from embarrassment. For a moment, nobody spoke. Brad thought maybe the girls were going to turn them down. Emily and Anna's dad was the one who finally broke the silence. "They seem like two solid young men. I think you girls need to take them up on their offer," he said.

So thanks to Emily and Anna's father, Brad and Brent had dates with girls who, at that moment, were the two most desired ladies on the grounds of Carson-Newman's campus. The boys called a couple of days after that to confirm their plans, and the Patton girls were going to be having themselves a date.

Chapter 4

The Friday night before Allison left for the beach was a rare evening when neither of her children were at a friend's house or had a ballgame. She used it as an opportunity to spend some quality time with Cicilly and Garret.

Their night was to begin with grilling burgers on the patio, and then they would move the fun indoors. Once inside, they would bake brownies, microwave a bag of popcorn and watch a movie.

Gary had been invited to join the fun, but as usual, he managed to blow off his wife and kids. He made an appearance and then quickly scurried off to his basement. After Allison grilled the cheeseburgers, Gary ran outside, put a burger and some chips on a paper plate and told them he had to get some care packages ready to mail by morning.

"Would you like for me and the kids to come down and help you after we eat?" Allison asked, even thought she knew what Gary would probably say.

"No, that's okay," he answered. "My parents are going to bring some stuff over to go in the packages in a little bit. They'll help me fill them."

Allison, Cicilly and Garret knew what all that meant. Their dad would disappear until bedtime. Gary's parents would spend about five minutes with the kids, then go down to the basement with Gary. They would spend about five more minutes with the kids before they would leave to go home.

Allison and the kids were not going to let Gary and his parents cast their gloom over the night. It was a night of precious time together, and they were going to enjoy it.

While they ate their dinner, Allison and the kids talked about her leaving the next morning. She was worried that her kids would be a bit bummed their mom was going to the beach for a week while they were stuck at home. She even considered taking them out of school to go on the trip with her, but the month of May was full of state mandated tests, the distribution of yearbooks and other end-of-the-year school stuff. It was the worst possible time to take her kids out of school.

It came as a relief to Allison to find out both of her kids were getting excited about the prospect of spending some time with their dad. Before Mitch's death, Gary was the ever-present father, attending all of the kids' ballgames and dance recitals. Between his job and collecting things for items for "Love, Mitch," Gary scarcely ate a meal with his kids. They long gave up on the idea that he would again attend all of their activities.

The kids suffered a great deal of loss. Cicilly and Garret took it hard when Mitch died. Garret, who idolized his Uncle Mitch, was especially affected by the loss. It was hard to say whether Garret was more hurt by the passing of his favorite uncle or by the sudden absence of his dad.

Before she committed to going on the beach trip Allison got Gary's word he would take some vacation time from his job and a break from "Love, Mitch." He promised to devote himself entirely to his children while Allison was gone.

"I won't leave them with my parents or your parents," he said. I will not drop them off at friends' houses. They will be with me. When they are not at school, Cicilly and Garret will be bonding with dear ole Dad. They'll be sick of me by the time the week is over."

Allison hoped that time with his kids would make Gary fall in love with family time again. Cicilly and Garret did nothing wrong, yet their dad had pulled away from them. They needed their daddy so desperately. If he could just reconnect with the kids, things could begin to get better.

Cicilly and Garret were at the doorstep of their tween years. At best, Allison could expect some moodiness, back-talking and rebellion. If Gary continued staying so absent from his kids' lives, Allison feared they might be in for some major acting out in upcoming years. It would only be so long before their sadness over how distant their dad became would turn to anger. Allison put too much work into raising her children to allow that to happen.

She was worried about Garret the most. Her son had so identified with his Uncle Mitch from an early age. When Garret was three, he told Gary and Allison that he wanted to "be a Marine someday like Uncle Mitch."

Ever since proclaiming his goal to join the military, Garret had worn his hair in a flattop. Mitch told Garret it was "high and tight like a real Jarhead."

Without Mitch or Gary actively participating in his life, Allison was concerned about his lack of male role models. Allison felt like even with all that she was single-handedly taking on, there was still a void in her son's life she could never fill.

Allison was just as concerned about Cicilly. With her mass of pale blond curls, button nose and big, expressive blue eyes and full, rosy cheeks; it was easy to see that Cicilly was well on her way to becoming a knockout.

It would not be long before boys would be wanting to date her. Allison worried that Gary's absence would send Cicilly to look for love from other males.

Back when she was in college at East Tennessee State University, Allison had a professor for her child development class who mentioned a "sacrificial lamb" theory. That professor theorized that, in most dysfunctional families, one person would become the "sacrificial lamb." That is, the person who would take on all of the family's problems and act out in some way. Acting out could include things like becoming depressed, substance abuse and breaking the law. The "sacrificial lamb" let other family members off the hook because their problems became the focus, allowing other members of the family to ignore their own maladaptive behaviors.

Allison could never allow Cicilly or Garret to become "sacrificial lambs." Gary was the member of the family who was bringing them all down. Their kids' lives would not be ruined because he refused to see how distorted his own life had become.

Chapter 5

Monique had to plan her trip to the woods very carefully. Bo was very meticulous and detail-oriented. Every item in their storage shed had a very specific place. If things were out of sorts, he would notice.

Bo was meticulous like that. When he dressed to work on his farm, he always wore his shirt tucked into his Carhart jeans and a brown leather belt. When his day's work was complete, Bo hosed off his work boots and scrubbed his hands and nails until not a trace of dirt was left.

Bo's habit of neatness made Monique's mission all the more tricky.

Knowing she did not have much time, Monique changed into some old overalls and rubber boots she liked to wear when she went out to the farm with Bo. The shovel was in the corner of their garden shed. Monique made careful note of the spot, because that is where the shovel was always kept. Monique would have to clean it up after she was done. The shovel was washed off after every use, never put back with dirt caked on it.

Monique had placed the DVD back in the padded envelope and then wrapped it in a plastic bag. There was an insane madness to what Monique was doing. A DVD was not indestructible. She could smash it to bits, scratch it to the point that it could not be viewed or toss it in a fire. Any of those methods would be far more efficient than what she was doing.

In the back of her mind, Monique wanted to have an option to change her decision. She knew that she might still want to watch the DVD. If her conscience persisted to nag her, she might have to tell Bo about the tape. Burying rather than destroying the tape would allow Monique to dig it up if she ever changed her mind.

Monique felt like a madwoman on a crime spree as she grabbed Bo's shovel. She knew her actions were so crazy, yet she could not help herself. The urge to bury that tape in the ground was something she could not ignore. As much as she tried to purge the thought from her mind, it kept tumbling round and round. It was her wish that burying the tape might bury her bad thoughts.

An urge to keep looking over her shoulder bugged Monique as she walked into the woods behind her house with a shovel and the mysterious tape wrapped in plastic. *There will be no way to explain this if Bo comes home early*, Monique thought of herself.

She could not think of a good story to tell Bo if he were to catch her. She almost chuckled out loud when she imagined herself trying to convince him she had decided to make a time capsule to bury in the woods. Never, ever would Bo be gullible enough to believe that. There was no story good enough to cover her if she were to get caght.

Monique kept looking all around, her senses on high alert. Besides worrying about Bo seeing her, she was also concerned she might by spotted by a nosy neighbor. One nosy neighbor in particular might be a problem. Francine lived in the neighborhood. She was a Hen who did not hold Monique in the highest esteem.

"If Francine sees me going into the woods with a shovel, she'll surely ask about it. She's so nosy, it would drive her insane to see this and not ask questions," Monique mumbled to herself.

Monique ducked her head down as if that would keep anyone watching from knowing who she was. *I should have worn a hat. That would have disguised me*, she thought to herself.

Once she dug a hole that was about a six inches deep and twelve inches wide, Monique put the plastic bag containing the tape inside of the hole and quickly covered it back up. She patted down the dirt to make it look like nothing was disturbed. Monique found a large, flat rock to mark the spot, in case she ever decided to go back and dig it up.

Chapter 6

Emily and Anna never spent so long getting ready to go somewhere. In a drastic departure from the norm, they curled their hair and put on pink lip gloss. Erica and Rhonda teamed up to do the mini-minimalist-makeover.

Emily and Anna called out to their friends for help, but requested two considerations. The first was their make-up would be very light, as to not look like they really had any on at all. Stipulation number two was their hair would not be cut, colored, permed or otherwise altered in a lasting way.

Erica dusted their cheeks with blush, curled their eyelashes, swept an ivory powder over their faces and applied light pink lip gloss. Rhonda washed and dried their hair, then used a flat iron to make their tresses poker straight.

A look in the mirror left Emily and Anna very pleased. The makeover only enhanced their look of pristine innocence. Their pink lips, blush-swept cheeks and silky hair looked absolutely angelic.

Putting them in stylish outfits presented more of a challenge. Most of Emily and Anna's clothes were homespun; designed and sewn by their own hands. Their dresses were extremely modest, grazing their ankles and loosely flowing. Rhonda and Erica talked them into going a little shorter with the skirts and a bit more fitted overall.

Rhonda had the girls look through some fashion magazines and catalogs to find current looks that could be adapted to respect their modesty. In the end, the girls decided they could go to skirts that hit the top of their knees.

They stayed up all night cutting and sewing skirts to wear on their date. Emily made herself a brown and pink patchwork style skirt. She topped it off with a pink T-shirt from her closet and accessorized with brown sandals and a chunky brown wooden bracelet borrowed from Rhonda.

Anna made quite a bold color choice for a Patton girl by making her skirt from an orange and turquoise flowered fabric. On top, she wore a turquoise cap-sleeved blouse. Her own turquoise ballet flats and Erica's silver and turquoise necklace completed Anna's outfit.

Once they were ready for their date, Emily and Anna had to get their parents' approval of their new look. The girls were nervous about letting their parents see them all dolled up. They were not sure their mom and dad would approve of their concessions to vanity.

When their mom got tears in her eyes, they feared that she did not approve. The tears were not from disapproval, but disbelief. Their mom could not believe her twin little girls were grown women. It was a fact that could not be denied as they stood in front of her looking so polished and beautiful.

"Girls, I can't get over how pretty you two look," she said. I might need to get Erica and Rhonda to work on me."

Their daddy was afraid he might be losing his little twins. "Girls, those boys are going to take one look at you two and be ready to run off for a double wedding," he half joked.

When Brad and Brent rang the doorbell, their dad went to answer the door. Since they had already met at the reception, no introductions had to be made. "Hello Brad and Brent, so nice to see you again. Come on in," he said.

Brad immediately began complimenting the Patton's home. "I love your home, Mr. Patton. It's very welcoming."

When the boys came into the living room, Emily and Anna were sitting on the couch with their mom. Rhonda and Erica had been given very specific orders to stay in the back of the house. The girls did not want Brad and Brent to know they had enlisted help in getting ready.

When the girls stood up, the boys stood speechless for a moment. It was Brad who spoke first. "You girls look even more beautiful than when we saw you at Carson-Newman," he said.

Brent stood back behind his brother, looking shy and nodding his head.

There was something about Brad's comment that made Mr. Patton a little uneasy. It was a compliment that seemed a little bold to make in front of he and his wife on Brad's first visit to their home. Earlier when Brad walked in, he immediately complimented their home. It did not seem genuine, but like some automatic response that he thought he should say. The Patton home was nice, but it was extremely modest; nothing that would normally elicit a response. Something about that kid seemed overly confident and insincere. Mr. Patton much preferred Brent's shyness to Brad's boldness.

Brad kind of reminded Mr. Patton of a Smooth Sam in training. Sam White had the biggest car lot in Langrid. When he first began with a small used car lot, Sam was already slightly over-the-top. Every year, as Sam became more successful, he got more flashy and boastful. He became a caricature of the sleazy used car dealer. Every word that Sam spoke was picked from his collection of gimmicks and annoying slogans.

Brad seemed to know all the tricks and all the right words, but nothing about him came off as genuine. Mr. Patton had an instinct many fathers possessed. He could spot a devil in disguise. Watching his wife and daughters swoon as Brad spilled trite compliments made Mr. Patton wonder if the ladies in his family would ever clue into the real Brad.

Chapter 7

Marlene made an early morning visit to Cutie Pies before leaving for her beach trip. She expected to find the place empty at that time of morning, but Adam was already in the kitchen hard at work.

Adam was wearing his apron that looked like a checkered racing flag. A perk for the Cutie Pies employees was the huge selection of cute aprons Marlene provided. When Adam came on board, Marlene had to order some more masculine choices. Adam's choices included aprons decorated with pictures of bass, vintage cars, baseballs and camoflauge.

"Good morning, Marlene. I didn't expect to see you here today," he said.

"Oh, I just wanted to come by and make sure everything was in order before I left for my trip. You guys need anything before I go?" she asked.

"Nope, we'll miss our fearless leader, but I think we'll be fine," he answered.

Marlene felt almost silly saying she had to check on things. She knew good and well Adam alone could take care of Cutie Pies. With the Charity's leadership and the Patton twins pitching in to do whatever was needed, everything was more than covered. The bakery would be run perfectly.

Adam wanted to assure his boss her business would be taken care of.

"Marlene, you know we'll work this place like it's our own," he said. "Just go and have a good time. You have absolutely nothing to worry about."

"I know, and Adam, I am so thankful I can leave and know everything will be okay around here," she said. "One of these days, I'll quit being such a control freak."

Adam tended to be quite direct. He had not always been that way. Like many good Virginia farm boys, Adam was raised to never say things that made people feel bad or uncomfortable. Then, Adam moved to Detroit for a job in the auto industry. He learned pretty quickly that his small town ways were going to get him eaten alive in the big city. His wit and tongue became sharp enough to hang with the hardest of big city folk.

Adam was not rude by any stretch of the imagination. In fact, he was quite the gentleman. While not rude, Adam was direct. Some people's conversations were so rolled up in small talk that it is hard to understand their point. Adam had a name for those kinds of conversations. Those conversations are like Blow Pops. The main reason anyone wants to eat a blow pop is to get to the bubble gum in the center; but you have to lick lots of sugar to get there. Adam bit down right to the bubble gum center. He cut out most of the small talk so that his point was never lost. He decided to go out on a limb and ask Marlene a question that was begging to be addressed.

"Are you worried about the new Walmart Supercenter?" he asked.

Marlene did not have to think very long before answering Adam's question. "I'm a little anxious, but sort of excited about having a new challenge," she said. Besides, it's going to be convenient for me to have a Walmart so close. I won't be running to Langrid all the time to buy shampoo and laundry detergent. I can't complain about Walmart coming to town when I'm going to be in there as much as anybody else. If I'm not opposed enough to inconvenience myself by not shopping there, then I guess I can't really consider myself in opposition of it coming to town."

The town of Coleman was abuzz with news that a Walmart supercenter was being built just ten minutes outside of the city limits. It was not a big surprise to anyone. A section of interstate with an exit ramp leading to Coleman was almost complete. Even though she knew the road project would probably bring in competition for her bakery, Marlene never fought the progress. Actually, she did quite the opposite. Marlene and her parents decided to sell her grandparents' farm when a developer became interested in that property after the highway project was announced. Marlene willingly participated and benefited from progress and change in her town.

Selling the farm was a difficult decision. Money was the biggest factor. Marlene and her parents received enough from the sale to allow her parents a very comfy retirement. Marlene used the money to expand the square footage of the bakery, hire employees and refurbish the rooms over the bakery to make the daycare room for the children and a real estate office for her husband Mark.

Marlene was almost certain her grandparents would have been happy with their decision. Without her grandmother and grandfather, there never would have been a Cutie Pies. The business began in her grandmother's kitchen. Their first pies were filled with fruits and berries her grandparents grew on their farm. Even the name of the business came from Marlene's grandfather calling her "Cutie Pie" as a nickname when she was growing up. When Marlene's grandfather passed away, it was his life insurance money that paid for a building to house their growing pie business. In one way or another, Marlene's grandfather had always taken care of his family. Even after his death, he was still ensuring them a better life. The sale of the land brought more money than they could ever make farming the land. In a way, it was a commentary on the sad state of people trying to make a profit on family-run farms. In the end, the farm had taken care of the family, just in a different way than originally intended.

The money was great, but it was not the only reason Marlene embraced the changes coming to her hometown. Marlene believed in her pies. She felt confident Cutie Pies offered better pies than anywhere else. Sure, people would go to the supercenter to get cookies and cakes. They would even pick up pies when they did not have the time to make a special trip to her bakery. Deep down, Marlene had confidence that when people wanted something special for dessert, they would still be coming to her. Marlene welcomed a chance to prove herself. She would be naïve not to think the new store might not affect her business, but she was going to work hard to prove that she could go up against a corporate giant and still survive. After all, Marlene's favorite Bible story had always been the tale of David versus Goliath.

Everyone had heard all kinds of horror stories about Walmart coming into town and driving out the little guys. Marlene had to be somewhat concerned but refused to become alarmed. A stop at Cutie Pies was part of the weekly routine for at least half the folks in Coleman. Cutie Pies was part of Coleman's culture and had become intertwined in the traditions of most of Coleman's families. Many Thanksgivings were not complete without Indian Pudding pie from Cutie Pies. Gretchen Harlow would not think of celebrating her birthday without one of Marlene's Scarlet Lady pies. Gretchen said she would rather go out in a thin skirt with no slip than see a birthday pass without that crimson red pie. There had not been a church pot luck, club meeting or family reunion occur in the town for the past twenty years that did not feature one of Marlene's pies. Walmart was big business and convenience. Cutie Pies was part of the fabric of the town. Marlene refused to believe that fabric would become easily unraveled. There was a certain status to serving a pie from

Cutie Pies. There was a little history and lots of pride baked into every pie. Each and every pie was a loving tribute to Marlene's grandmother. That kind of pride could not be mass produced. Would the people of Coleman pay a little extra for a pie with a little love baked into it? Marlene was banking on the fact they would. There was an intangible value to a pie crust rolled out by hand using an old wooden rolling pin. If the nostalgia and tradition were not enough to keep people coming, Marlene had another idea up her apron. Once she returned from the beach, she was going to put in place a plan that would put her on the forefront of a brand new trend.

Marlene was the first person in her area to market giant pies with ornate garnishes and unique fillings for wedding and other fancy occasions. The special occasions pies were still selling like crazy. A new food craze would soon be making a debut in Coleman. Her imagination was the incubator for an incredibly smart idea that would soon hatch into a master plan. Marlene knew she would begin making her new plan a reality when she returned from her beach trip. She told nobody but her husband. She predicted her new idea would cause an increase in business, even with the new Walmart coming. Coleman was her town and Walmart would not keep her from remaining queen of the pie business!

Chapter 8

Allison stared in disbelief at the back of her minivan. "Since I've had kids I've never gone an hour away from my house with one bit less than we've got packed in the back of this van right now. Are you girls sure we've got everything? This doesn't look like much. When we go on a family vacation, we can barely close the hatch on the back of my van because of all of our stuff."

Dorothy was certain after checking and rechecking everyone's list, there was no way anything they needed for the beach was being left behind. "Allison, you know how much I've mulled over our lists," she said. "There are no diaper bags, no Pack-N-Plays, portable swings, travel high chairs or any of that other stuff that takes up a bunch of room. It's just us girls for the week. We're child-free, husband-free and schedule-free."

Marlene recalled a beach trip from many years ago. "Hey, the last beach trip we had together was when we went down to Myrtle Beach for Senior Week after high school graduation," she said.

Allison looked around before speaking to make sure all the precious ears of her children were out of hearing range. Allison was not exactly a wild child during her teen years, but she did present a few challenges for her parents she did not want Cicilly and Garret to repeat for her. Any hint she had not been the most perfect angel as a teenager was carefully hidden from her children. It was not that Allison made a habit of lying to her kids, but she became very skilled at omitting details. She likened it to when people wipe off their kitchen counter, but do not get into the corners. Anyone giving it a quick glance would think the counter is all shiny and clean. A closer look and moving around some items could reveal a not-so-clean surface. "I wipe off the surface for my kids, hoping that they never start looking into the corners."

Senior Week at Myrtle Beach was a rite of passage taken by hoards of kids all across the Southeast. Scads of recent gradu-ates flocked to the South Carolina town full of sun, surf and cheap hotels. The teens' days would be spent on the beach or by the pool. At night, they would pack into dance clubs. The whole week was drenched in the most inexpensive beer that could be bought. Kids who towed the line and lived a whole-some existence all through high school would turn into over-sexed boys and hot little hoochies, powered by cheap alcohol and the freedom of being away from home without any paren-tal supervision. There was strict unspoken code that the events that occurred during this week, after walking across the gradu-ation stage, were not supposed to follow the graduates back to their hometowns. All the crazy partying and lewd acts would be chalked up to the depravity of Senior Week.

One or two kids would always crack. They would tell someone the secrets of Senior Week. The stories would be out and spread all around town. Senior Weeks' most extraordinary incidents would become legend. Some parents used these legends as basis for not letting their kids go to Senior Week. Others let their kids go but not before retelling the tales to warn their children of the dangers and temptations they were about to face. It was with many lectures and warnings that Allison, Marlene and Dorothy's parents sent them to the beach.

Allison, Marlene and Dorothy had packed into Allison's little Mazda the morning after their graduation ceremony. The car was so cramped that the girls had to pack all of their stuff in plastic bags instead of suitcases. About a hundred plastic grocery bags were stuffed all over that Mazda; in every little nook and cranny, under the seats, on the dash and all along the rear window.

The hotel room the girls rented matched the shabbiness of their plastic bag luggage. It was theirs for the week; thirty-five dollars per night, two double beds, a bathroom and cable television. The room smelled like smoke, the bathtub had a constant drip that made for nights of sleepless water torture and the carpet wore stains from senior weeks past.

Allison, the neat freak, immediately walked to the supermarket across the street to buy cleaning supplies. Dorothy, in her need to protect her friends' welfare, made sure that the deadbolt on the door and the window locks were in working order. "My mom saw a story on the news about how dangerous staying in hotel rooms can be," she said. "Scads of people have been attacked by intruders in their hotel rooms."

By that time, Allison was pouring bleach into the toilet. "The biggest danger in this place is bacteria. It is na-steee!" she exclaimed.

Marlene, the girl who was full of ideas of what they would be doing on their trip, wanted to let the fun begin. She was eyeing her new red bikini she just laid out on the bed and tried to refocus her friends' attention to the real purpose of their trip. "Girls, we gotta get our bathing suits on, grab our beach towels and get out there. Did you all see all those tags from different states on cars in the parking lot? There are guys from all over the place down here just waiting to meet three pretty girls. Then, we can come in, get cleaned up and go somewhere good to eat."

Marlene coaxed her friends out of their icky room and onto the sand. A mere fifteen minutes after the girls had begun basking on the beach, it began to rain. Allison tried to rally her friends' optimism with her prediction the rain would not set in.

"Rain showers pass over quickly at the beach," she said. This isn't like home, where the mountains can trap it in. Ten minutes from now, the sun will be out again."

Dorothy, the sobering voice of reason with a slightly apologetic tone, was quick to pop Allison's sunny little bubble. "I'm sorry to tell you, but according to the weather forecast, this week could be a complete washout. It's supposed to rain every day."

As they gathered up their towels and suntan lotion, Marlene came in with a plan to pass the time while it rained. "We can go to the mall and shop for a while, eat a good dinner, come back and get ready to go out," she suggested.

The three girls found the closest shopping mall. They shopped for clothes, got ice cream and shopped some more. By late afternoon, they were stuffing at least a dozen shopping bags into Allison's little car.

After going back to their room for two hours of primping, they went out to dinner. Marlene's palate and passion for good food was well-developed by that time. She heard about a seafood restaurant she wanted to try. "Hey, there's this place up in Murrell's Inlet called Drunken Jack's," she said. "The Wilsons who live next door to us ate there last summer and said it's so good."

The girls drove to Murrell's Inlet so they could try Drunken Jack's famous hush puppies. While waiting for their table, they hung out at the lounge on a dock that overlooked the water. They met up with some cute boys from Georgia who pretended to be in college even though they were also fresh out of high school. The girls felt very sophisticated when the boys brought them strawberry daiquiris. After Allison finished her daiquiri, she decided to order another. "I'll carry my glass up to the bar and ask for another drink. If the bartender sees that I already have had one, he'll think I'm legal," she reasoned.

Who did Allison think she was kidding? With her cheerleader ponytail tied up in a big bow and a T-shirt that read "Class of 1985," she was hardly passing for legal drinking age, which was twenty at that time in South Carolina. Allison sat her empty glass on the bar and said, "I'd like another." The bartender's assistant asked, "Do you and your friends all want another round?"

By the time they got halfway through with round two of their drinks, the girls were acting sufficiently drunk. They were laughing way too loudly, singing to every song that came on over the speakers and flirting so much that several girls were ready to fight them over their men.

Allison was feeling so good. She felt the need to pay a compliment to the bartender. "Boy, you mix up some stout strawberry daiquiris," she said.

Some seasoned drinkers were sitting around the bar when Allison made her comment. The men got a huge kick out of a petite little thing declaring a strawberry daiquiri as a "stout" drink. "Hey cutie, I'll show ya stout. How 'bout a Jack and Coke or a shot of whiskey?"

The man's proposal frightened Allison. In the world of drinking, she was pathetically lightweight. Besides the occasional sips of wine her parents shared with her on rare occasions, that night had been her first foray into alcohol. She wondered how she was going to save face in front of the people who heard the man making fun of her. "Uh, I don't know,"she said. One of us girls is going to have to drive back home. We probably ought to quit now so we'll be sober in a few hours."

At that point the bartender began to laugh. "Cutie, you and your friends don't have to worry about how you're going to get home," he mused.

Was the bartender propositioning her? It may have been the daiquiris boosted her confidence, but Allison concluded she and her friends were the cutest girls in the place. Was the much older, but very cute bartender offering to give her a ride home? With about thirty people standing around to see the exchange, Allison turned up the flirtation. "If we're still around when you get off work, I might just let you give me a ride home."

Allison was mortified by the words that came out of her mouth. Her mother and father always warned her about getting in cars with strangers. If it really came right down to it, she would have to figure out a way to get out of letting the bartender take her home. Jumping in the car with some guy she never met was a quick way to become a Myrtle Beach Senior Week Statistic.

Myrtle Beach Senior Week Statistics were unofficial figures on the number of girls who got into bad situations during the week. They were basically urban legends parents used to add scientific-sounding validity to the stories that warned their kids about all of the bad things that could happen if their behavior got out of hand.

Allison would soon find the bartender was not flirting with her and the only Myrtle Beach Statistic she was becoming was in the "girls who come down here and act dumb" category. "Sweetheart," the bartender continued. "You don't have to worry about how you and your friends are going to get home because your drinks don't have any alcohol in them. Those boys who bought you drinks sent over virgin daiquiris. They weren't old enough to order alcohol, and you're not old enough to drink it."

Lots of people were standing around the bar. Most had been listening to the conversation between Allison and the bartender. The overall mood around the bar was one of suppressed laughter. They wanted to burst out laughing but sensed Allison's humiliation.

Allison did not know whether to laugh or cry. In the moment, she was completely embarrassed, especially because so many people were looking at her. She also knew that by the end of the trip, she and her friends would be laughing about how silly they had been.

It was not in spunky Allison style to walk away with her head hanging down in shame. "Well, in that case, pour us a round of waters. We might as well not be paying for high dollar drinks if they don't pack a punch."

Allison may have come off as a flakey teeny-bopper, but at least she was adorable. All of the folks around the bar felt free to release their pent-up chuckles after Allison staged her cute comeback. Her dad had always told her, "People love a good sport."

Her dad's advice had sure helped her that night. Her sense of humor charmed even the bartender who had so publicly humiliated Allison. "Hey, you and your friends can have your fill of water, soft drinks and tea on the house all night long. And if you weren't so young I would be trying to give you a ride home," he said.

Later in the night, when the bartender sent a round of Shirley Temples, Allison tied her maraschino cherry stem in a knot with her tongue, placed her it on a napkin and sent it back to the bartender via their waitress. "He made me blush. Now I'm going to do the same to him."

Allison may have been a lightweight drinker, but she was also a hardcore flirt.

When Allison returned to her friends carrying glasses of water, Dorothy assumed the bartender had cut them off. "Did he tell you we couldn't have any more drinks because we're so buzzed?" she asked.

Marlene was afraid their being underage had been discovered. "Did he ask to see your ID? Is he calling the cops?" she asked.

Allison explained what happened. The girls were shocked to find they had been acting like tipsy lushes while stone-cold sober. At first, Dorothy was so embarrassed she wanted to leave the restaurant. "Let's just go somewhere else to eat," she said.

Marlene was not in agreement. "I will not go home without eating at Drunken Jack's," she said. "This is the main thing I want to do down here."

Dorothy gave in to Marlene's demands and remained at the restaurant. "Well, I guess we might as well stay here. We've already been waiting over an hour for a table. If we go somewhere else, Lord knows when we might get to eat."

The girls munched on baskets of the famous Drunken Jack's hush puppies and honey butter while they were waiting for their table. The hush puppies did little to take the edge off their appetites. They were all quite hungry by the time they were seated at a table. They ordered appetizers, large entrees and desserts. When the bill came, they were in for a bit of sticker shock. Although the dinner was more than they expected, the girls did not shortchange their waitress. "Fifteen percent," Dorothy said.

"You should always tip a waiter or waitress at least fifteen percent," she said. "My parents told me tipping anything less for good service is just rude. Even Pastor Harper mentioned being a good tipper one time in a sermon. Pastor Harper worked as a waiter in a restaurant when he was in college. He said sadly, Sunday was the worst day of his week. He also said many of the Sunday customers were overly demanding, impatient and cheap tippers. He declared he never wanted to hear of anybody from our church going to a restaurant on Sunday, or any other day of the week, and mistreating our server. He said if we wanted to be good Christian witnesses, we had no business leaving church, then acting ugly towards somebody trying to do their job. My parents took that sermon as a challenge. There were a few times before he listened to that sermon that my dad had gotten angry over having to wait too long to be seated or left a bad tip because he thought the restaurant was overpriced. Never, ever again was Dad anything but a polite customer and a great tipper."

Too bad Dorothy did not pay as much attention to all of her parents' financial advice. A day of shopping and a nice dinner left all of the girls short on cash. Dorothy discovered her financial straits while balancing her check book in the car on their way to a dance club. She counted the money in her wallet, hoping there was an extra twenty stashed somewhere.

"Hey girls, I spent too much today," she said. "I'm going to be way short on cash."

Allison knew she and Dorothy began the trip with roughly the same amount of money. They babysat for months to save up money for their trip. "Hey Dorothy, I'm probably as broke as you are. Do you care to get in my purse and look at my checkbook and count the money that's left in my wallet?" Allison said.

While Allison drove, Dorothy sized up her money situation. They began discussing solutions to their problem. All along the road there were signs advertising bikini and wet T-shirt contests with cash prizes. Allison and Dorothy talked about the possibility of that being their source of money.

Dorothy assessed her assets. "Well, the bikini contest is out for me. I usually won't even wear a two-piece out on the beach. I sure won't be wearing one in a night club."

Allison considered what her physique had to offer. "Well, I look okay in a bikini in a teeny-bopper kind of way. I have no boobs to speak of."

Dorothy decided the two of them combined might have the winning combination. "I do have boobs. Unfortunately, I have the tummy, behind and thighs to go with the big boobs. If we put my boobs on your body, we'd be in business. We could go to a different contest every night and win every prize they have."

Allison knew who had the best sum total of all body parts. "I think Marlene should have to enter the contests. She has the perfect figure."

Marlene thanked Allison for the compliment, but passed on the opportunity to display her flesh to a mob of rowdy eighteen-year-old boys. "I don't think any of us are the types of girls that would feel okay doing those contests. We turn our backs to each other when we change clothes. How in the world would we stand up half naked in front of hundreds of people?" she asked.

Dorothy agreed. "It would be a pretty cheap thing to do."

Allison knew they were right. "I'd feel embarrassed to do something like that, and my parents would die if they ever found out. Knowing my luck, if I did a contest like that, someone from

Coleman would be in the crowd to take my picture. Then everyone in town would know. I'd just die! It would be more embarrassing than Jolie Greene's topless catastrophe."

One of the most infamous stories of bad things that happened during Senior Week was Jolie Greene's topless sunbathing mishap. Jolie graduated from high school a couple of years before. On her senior beach trip, she had her first alcoholic beverages right before going out on the beach to tan with her girlfriends.

Her friend Patty had mixed up a pitcher of purple hooter shooters. As inexperienced drinkers, the girls did not realize "shooter" meant the drink was of a strength that was meant to be shot from tiny shot glasses, not sucked through straws from giant plastic tumblers. By the time the pitcher was finished, Jolie and friends were sufficiently trashed. They stumbled out to the beach to sunbathe and sleep-off their drunkenness. The girls laid their beach towels, oiled up and passed out.

Right before she plopped down on her tummy to sun her back, Jolie undid the strings on her two-piece. When she first closed her eyes, Jolie felt like the beach was spinning, which made her swear that she would never drink again.

Instead of the horrible spinning, Jolie began to focus on the sound of the ocean waves. Before long, she had drifted into a deep, drunken sleep. At some point during that deep sleep, Jolie, unaware of where she was or of the fact that her top was undone, rolled over to her back.

It was a cruel irony that Jolie had irresponsibly over consumed a beverage with "hooter" in its name. The effects of that drink led to her showing her hooters to everyone on the beach.

Jolie rolled just as a group of boys from their school were walking by. Careful not to wake Jolie, or her sleeping girlfriends, one of the boys began quietly snapping photos of her while she was in an open-mounted, dead to the world, passed out state with her top half fully exposed.

Jolie's open-mouthed, dead to the world state did not make for a super-sexy *Playboy* type of photo. Instead, she could have been the subject of a poster for warning against alcohol's ill-effects with a "Don't be this girl!" caption.

Kevin Rich was the boy who took photos of Jolie. He was with a group of five other guys. One of the boys, Ryan Counts, had a big crush on Jolie. He knew that she was a nice girl who had just gotten a little careless during Senior Week. Fortunately, Ryan seized Kevin's camera, and took the film out. Ryan lost Kevin as a friend but gained Jolie as a girlfriend. The pictures never made it to Coleman, but the story did.

Marlene had a more practical solution to their problem. While Dorothy and Allison had been up front talking, Marlene was in the back seat counting how much money she had left. Marlene had a little more than her friends. By that time, she and her grandmother had been selling lots of friend pies and coffee at the county stockyard on Saturday mornings.

Marlene made a generous offer. "Okay, let's pool our money and see how much we have for the week."

At first, Allison and Dorothy refused to let Marlene cover them with her extra money. Marlene finally found a way to win them over. "Hey, if I'm the only one with any money then I'd have to go out by myself. That's not going to happen. How much fun could it possibly be to go out by myself? I'll just wind up hanging out in the room at night with you two. So, are we going to hang out in the room all week, starving and miserable, or will you guys let me help you out so we can have fun?"

Marlene's money was not enough to cradle them in the lap of luxury. By the end of the week, they had bought a box of Pop Tarts, a loaf of bread, a jar of peanut butter, a bag of potato chips and one bunch of bananas to sustain them through breakfast, lunch and dinner until they got home.

Marlene was sure they would not run out of money on their second beach trip. "We've got a little more cash at our disposal this time. If that runs out, we've got plastic. As long as we don't lose our credit cards, we'll be just fine!" she said.

Dorothy pulled a canvas tote full of food out of her car. "Just in case, I've made sure we have everything we need," she said.

Dorothy never went anywhere without having a bag full of snacks. In the tote, she had packed Pop Tarts, three loaves of her homemade sourdough bread, peanut butter, potato chips and bananas. "Thought I'd pack all of this for old time's sake. I remember thinking all of this stuff was pretty good for the three days we lived on it."

Marlene had already been dreaming of all the good food she would be eating on the trip. "Okay, you all can eat all the Pop Tarts and peanut butter sandwiches you want," she said. "I've gotta have some crab cakes and shrimp and grits while I'm in Hilton Head."

Dorothy was looking forward to eating a meal where the only person she had to worry about feeding was herself. "It has been forever since I've gotten to eat a meal right when the plate's been set in front of me. Usually, I'm so busy cutting up Darla's food and coaxing her to eat that I don't get to touch my meal until it has gotten cold. Most of the time, I wind up taking half my meal home in a box and taking it to work for lunch the next day."

Allison knew this would be the first trip in a long time that would truly be relaxing. "You know, after you have kids, you no longer take vacations. You take trips, but there is no such thing as a vacation when you're keeping up with kids. You have to do everything for your kids on vacation that you do for them at home."

As much as they would enjoy getting away from their daily routines, the ladies knew they would miss their families in a horrible way. Marlene cried for ten minutes when it came time to say goodbye to Alex that morning. Dorothy's husband joked he was going to have to use a crow-bar to break the embrace she had with Darla before she left their house. Even Allison's kids, who had reached an age where open affection with Mom was not so cool, had a sentimental moment in the driveway.

Cicilly and Garret's warm embraces were followed by Gary's passionless goodbye kiss. To Allison, it was like taking a big bite of cold oatmeal; worse than bland and almost sickening.

Right after Allison backed out of the driveway Dorothy made a prediction. "We're going on this trip to get some time away from home, but I bet we'll spend about eighty-percent of our time in Hilton Head talking and worrying about our kids and other stuff at home."

Chapter 9

The drive to Hilton Head began as uphill climbs, twists and turns as they crossed the mountains of North Carolina. Soon after crossing into South Carolina, they reached Spartanburg, where they made a little detour for lunch at Dorothy's in-law's house. Tom's mom had told Dorothy if they called in the morning when they left Coleman, she'd make them lunch.

Tom's mom, Elle, cooked all morning. By the time Dorothy and her friends arrived, she had food set out all over her kitchen counter. It was a hearty lunch that would hold them over until a late dinner.

Elle had fixed a huge platter of fried chicken, a bowl of pasta salad and a pan of yeast rolls. For dessert, she made banana pudding. What Dorothy was most looking forward to was Elle's pimiento cheese.

Elle made the most delicious pimiento cheese. She shredded the cheese herself, and like a true Carolinian, she never thought of using anything but Duke's Mayonnaise. Every meal at Elle's house included pimiento cheese. She spread it on sandwiches, stuffed it into cherry tomatoes, worked it into her bread dough and topped cheeseburgers and steaks with it. When Dorothy was battling cancer, Elle's pimiento cheese was one of the few things she could tolerate after her nauseating chemo treatments.

Elle noticed Dorothy's eyes were panning the countertop. "Don't worry. I'd never have my Dorothy over without making pimiento cheese. There's a big platter on the dining room table full of pimiento cheese finger sandwiches and celery stuffed with pimiento cheese. I'll pack whatever's left in plastic containers for you to take on your trip."

After lunch was set out on the table, Elle sat down with them to eat and catch up on how the girls were doing. Elle had gotten to know them all quite well because she often did extended stays in Coleman to help Dorothy when she was battling cancer.

Since Allison had walked in the house, Elle noticed she was not herself. "Allison, I think about your family so much. How are you all doing?" asked Elle.

"Well, the kids and I are pretty good. Gary's another story," said Allison.

Elle could tell Allison was deeply upset when she spoke Gary's name.

"Allison, I'm so sorry. I guess he's taking it pretty hard," said Elle.

"I knew this would be hard on Gary, but it's changed him. It's like it has robbed him of his soul. I think the kids and I could set ourselves on fire, and he might not notice. We're competing with Mitch's memory for Gary's attention," said Allison.

"I'm so sorry your family has had gone through this," said Elle. I lost my grandma on my mother's side when I was just ten years old. We were so close. She lived just a couple of houses down from us. I was used to seeing her every single day. She was like a second mother to me. When she died, it broke my heart so bad. I was a lost little girl.

"The worst part of the whole thing was my mom could barely function for about two years. Her mom was so much a part of her life that it was like my mom did not know who she was without my grandmother.

"After about two years, my mother finally emerged from her fog. The sadness would still hit her, but she wasn't sad all the time. She started going out and living like a normal person.

"What she went through, and what Gary might go through is a second wave of grief over all the things that were missed when she was so depressed. There were two years worth of holidays, birthdays, my brother's ballgames and my school plays she missed. Mom might have been physically present, but her mind was out of it. She had a real sense of regret and guilt when she realized how much she missed with me and my brother. The sooner you get Gary to snap to it, the better."

David, Tom's father, came by during his lunch hour to visit with the girls. He was a quiet man but no less warm and sweet as his wife. He got caught up on how they all were doing before he grabbed a quick lunch and headed back to his job.

Before he left, David made a point to offer some encouragement to Allison. "Girl, you gotta just hang in there," she said. "Gary's got a good woman in you. He's going to realize how great you are this week. One time, Elle went to visit her sister for a week and left me with the kids. I had a whole new respect for her when she got back in town. I hope to see you again soon, and I hope things get much better for you and Gary."

* * *

The girls had a hard time saying goodbye to Elle, but they needed to get back on the road. As Dorothy predicted, the three of them talked mostly about their kids on the ride to the beach. Dorothy posed the question, "Anybody else feel guilty about leaving their children? I should be thinking about nothing but relaxing at the beach with my friends and a good book, but my mind keeps going back to Darla. I'm worried she'll miss me and think I've abandoned her, or what if she doesn't miss me. That would hurt my feelings so bad. Oh, listen to me. I'm sounding selfish. I shouldn't want her to be sad about me being gone. I should want her to have a great week with her dad."

Marlene had the same feelings as Dorothy. "You know Dorothy, I think it's that we want to feel indispensible as moms. We may sometimes gripe and moan about how much work it is to take care of our families, but when it comes right down to it, I want to think nobody else can take care of Alex the way I can. I say I want everything to go great while I'm gone, but part of me hopes maybe Mark does find it a challenge to get all of the laundry done and still take care of Alex. I won't feel as useful if it all runs too smoothly for him. It's not like Mark doesn't help me around the house and with Alex. He does. He's a huge help, but we're kind of traditional. I take care of most of the inside chores while he does most of the man stuff, you know, yard work and home repairs. If he can do my job as well or better than I do it, I'm going to feel pretty bad about myself when I get home. I hope he's like Tom's dad and thinks I'm the greatest woman in the world when he has to do all of the stuff I do every day as a mom."

While her friends were worried their husbands might do too good a job taking care of things, Allison had the opposite worry. "I just hope Gary remembers to feed the kids," she said. "I swear if he doesn't snap out of it soon, I don't know what I'm going to do. Gary's grief over Mitch has just about sucked all of the life out of him. I literally feel like I'm living with a stranger. He's so closed off to me and the kids anymore. Sometimes I wonder if he still loves us or if he's so depressed he doesn't even care about anything anymore, including me and the kids."

Allison vented for about five minutes before the tears began to roll. When at first her friends did not say anything, Allison was afraid they were not sympathetic. "I know you all are probably thinking I'm so self-centered to be upset about my situation. There's no way I could be hurting as badly as Gary and his family. I probably seem like I'm just whining."

Marlene finally summoned up the nerve to verbalize something that she had been thinking for months. She hoped that it would not hurt Allison's feelings. "Allison, do you feel sort of shut out by Gary and his family?" she asked. You've mentioned how much time he spends with his parents on his "Love, Mitch" project. It's sort of like Gary and his parents are leaning on each other and leaving you out. You've said he's become emotionally unavailable. It sounds kind of like he might be emotionally unavailable to you and the kids, but not to his parents."

"Marlene, you are so right," said Allison. "I knew I was jealous of the time he was spending on the care packages, but I am completely eaten up with jealousy over the fact that Gary is sharing his feelings with his parents instead of me. I mean, I expect Gary to talk to them about Mitch. It's just that he talks only to them and never to me about it. Maybe Gary thinks I don't want to hear it, but I would so much rather see him screaming and crying than being so blank-faced and numbed-out. I would never, ever want to come between him and his parents, but the kids and I are supposed to be his first priority."

Dorothy confessed she was a little aggravated at Gary. "Allison, I have felt so terrible for Gary since this happened, but he's not being fair to you,"she said. "You are his wife, and you have tried to be supportive. You've been his partner and best friend. Gary needs to realize how hurtful it is for him to not include you in every aspect of his life, including his grief."

Talking things out with her friends helped Allison clarify what she had been denying to herself. "You know, I think I feel sort of disrespected that Gary is leaving me out of such an important thing that is going on in his life," she said. He ought to know I'm strong enough to shoulder some of his burden. It insults me if he thinks I can't handle it. I used to be a nurse. Of course I'm experienced in dealing with death and its aftermath."

It was such a relief for Allison to hear her friends tell her she had the right to be angry. Somehow the way Marlene and

Dorothy spoke about the situation made it seem more manageable. Every time Allison tried to discuss things with Gary, it came out as her thinking he needed to speed up his grieving process and get on with life. When Allison got home from the beach, she would simply ask Gary to rely a little more on her and share the same things with her that he was sharing with his parents. Allison knew Gary did not want to bog her down with his sadness, but not communicating with her was killing their relationship. Maybe the same argument presented in a different way would help Gary understand Allison's position.

Marlene asked Allison about Mitch's widow, Shelly. "How about Shelly and the kids? How are they doing?"

"They're as well as can be expected. Shelly seems to be doing better than Gary and his parents. Of course, Shelly doesn't see she has any choice but to go on and keep living. She's determined her kids won't grow up in a sad house. It's all up to her now, so she does what she has to. Shelly said she only allows herself fifteen minutes a day to think about being sad. The rest of the time, she's too busy to think about anything but raising her kids on her own. She's told the kids nobody in the house was allowed to be moping around all the time. They've tried to keep things pretty normal. The kids are still doing all of their activities. They have a family dinner together at the table at least four nights a week. I admire her for the way she's handled this. Shelly's been awfully strong for her kids. If only Gary could muster up that same kind of strength."

Chapter 10

Just past Spartanburg, the land began to flatten out. While rolling through South Carolina's state capital of Columbia, the ladies saw a row of palmetto tress, the state tree of South Carolina. Upon seeing the palmettos, Allison squealed like a kid. "Oh goody, I feel like I'm close to the beach when I see those," she said.

As the trip progressed southward into the Low country, the land became flatter, the soil became sandier, and every now and then, they would see a swamp.

By late afternoon, the ladies were pulling up to their condo. It was modern, spacious and only steps from the beach. Best of all, they were all staying there for free.

Dorothy wondered if the inside of the condo would look as nice as the outside. If Patsy had anything to do with the inside décor, it was probably going to look like a tacky room in a cheap Vegas motel. Patsy had a way of "Patsy-tizing" any space she touched. She loved anything metallic, mirrored, feathered or tasseled. In her mind, Dorothy had imagined the condo being done up like Caesar's Palace.

Patsy styled herself in the most depressing, frumpy way. Her dresses were huges masses of fabric with less tailoring than a potato sack. She wore her hair in a chin-length cut that she had styled once a week. Patsy's hair was sprayed and teased so much that it all moved as one giant piece when she stepped out into the wind. The flair and flash Patsy lacked in personal style was instead expressed in the way she decorated.

What awaited them inside was worse than what Dorothy had imagined. Patsy had gone with a beach-bling- tiki-hut theme for the condo. All of the upholstery and curtains were done in fabrics that looked like they came straight out of Don Ho's closet. Large tiki totems and plastic palms trees were propped in corners, and tiki masks hung on the walls. A coffee table made from bamboo held a hollowed out coconut shell filled with potpourri that smelled like suntan lotion. Brightly colored leis were hung over doorknobs and chair posts.

Allison looked around and said, "I feel like I'm at Disney's Polynesian Resort."

That was not an insult coming from Allison. She was a freak for Disney World. She and her family always stayed at Polynesian Resort when they went. If she could, Allison would take her kids twice a year.

All Marlene and Dorothy could do was laugh when they looked around inside. "Looks like Patsy found a going out a business sale at a tiki bar," Marlene said.

Dorothy always dreamed of a Hawaiian vacation. "Maybe this is a two-in-one vacation," she said. "Outside, it's Hilton Head. Inside, it's Hawaii."

Their surroundings were not exactly serene, but the ladies were still happy to be there. A free place to stay at the beach was nothing to sneeze at, even if they were expecting "Tiny Bubbles" to begin spontaneously playing at any moment.

* * *

Sorting out their suitcases was not a difficult task. Their various tastes were evidenced in their luggage. Dorothy had the standard black. All of her clothes and makeup fit neatly into one suitcase. Allison had her things packed in cute red luggage with white polka-dots. Her essentials for the trip took up a suitcase and an overnight bag. Marlene's clothes and makeup took up a regular-sized suitcase, a carry-on suitcase and an overnight bag. Inside her whimsical Betsy Johnson black and white leopard designer luggage was almost twice as many clothes as she would actually need for the trip.

The process of getting everything out of the car and put away took about an hour. After that, the first thing the ladies wanted to do was to walk out on the patio to see the beach. Marlene swore one whiff of fresh salt-tinged air could do her more good than a spa day or a session with a shrink. She considered bi-annual visits to her parents' house in Florida to be a necessity. "It's what keeps me sane," she said. My trips to the beach save me from having to take Xanax. I would be the boss from Hell, a hateful wife and a terrible mother without my trips to Florida. If health insurance companies would pick up the tab for vacations, they'd probably save a whole lot of money on mental health service reimbursements."

Allison took a good look at Marlene, wishing she could grab that immediate sense of peace and relaxation. "I don't feel it yet, but maybe a whole week down here will give me some new perspective,"she said. "At least I'm here and getting a break from all the stress at home. I just hope I don't go home to things being exactly like they were when I left."

Dorothy was convinced Allison's absence would be a good thing."Maybe a whole week without you will make Gary look at things from a different angle. I think having to take over responsibility for everything you're doing will force him out of his fog. He won't be able to stay gone or plant himself in front of the television."

Allison had a talk with her kids to make sure that would not be happening. "Oh, Cicilly and Garett will make sure he doesn't neglect them while I'm gone. They're as frustrated as I am. They swore that they would be relentless in keeping Gary actively engaged with them."

Once the sea air cleared away Marlene's stress, her thoughts quickly turned to food. "Hey, why don't we go to the grocery store so we'll be stocked up on food for the week?"

All of them had packed some food for the trip, so they did not need much. A quick run through the closest Publix had them stocked up on milk, eggs, orange juice, fresh vegetables for salads, sandwich meat, and some fruit. As soon as they got back and put up their groceries, Marlene's thoughts again turned to food. "Where are we going to eat dinner tonight?" she asked.

Allison was feeling kind of worn and weary from all the crying she had done in the car. She did not want to throw a wet blanket on the evening, but she was not up to getting ready and going out that night. "Hey girls, I don't want you two to stay in on account of me, but I'm just too tired to go out tonight," she said. "I think I'm in the mood to stay back here and order a pizza."

Dorothy was excited to be in Hilton Head but also a little tired from riding in the car all day long. "Hey, pizza sounds good to me. There's a pizza place across the street at the marina," she said. I'll walk over there and pick up a pizza to bring back here."

Marlene got on board the pizza wagon. "I think it would be cool to relax for a little bit, then take a walk out on the beach."

* * *

Marlene and Dorothy decided to walk across the street to get the pizza. Directly across from their condo was the popular Salty Dog Marina. The marina was a cute blue and red conglomeration of shops and restaurants.

During the summer high season, the marina would have been packed with people. The marina still was host to a good number of travelers, but it was far less crowded than it would be in a few weeks after kids got out of school.

There would be a short wait for their pizza, so Dorothy and Marlene sat and listened to a guy that was playing live music on the dock. One minute, they were relaxing in their chairs listening to Jimmy Buffett songs. The next thing they knew, the two women were whisked onstage with the performer. They must have looked so cute sitting there swaying back and forth while singing along that the singer picked them out of the audience. As he grabbed them each by the hand, he announced, "Every lead singer needs a couple of pretty ladies to sing back-up."

Suddenly, Marlene was coming head-to-head with one of her worst fears. Marlene was confident in her ability to do many things, except for singing. Usually seen as a pretty cool lady, Marlene totally lost cool points when she had to sing. She was completely tone deaf. At a young age, Marlene found out she could not sing and Dorothy could.

As a very young child, Marlene had imagined she could sing. In her mind, she was pitch-perfect; a virtual songbird. Like almost every other little girl in the world, she would practice singing along to her favorite songs on the radio, belting it out into her hairbrush-turned-microphone. In the girly-pink sanctity of her bedroom with her stuffed animals as her adoring audience, Marlene was a superstar. When the children's choir director at her church wanted volunteers for solos in the Christmas play, Marlene was the first to raise her hand.

Marlene grew up in a tiny church. There were only eight kids in the children's choir. Only three of them volunteered for solos. Because of the slim pickins, Mrs. Young, the children's choir director, had very realistic expectations about the quality of the solos featured in the Christmas program. She knew the program would never be a slick production of prodigious vocal talent. Instead it was a sweet display of the children's true joy of singing for their parents and extended church family. Mrs. Young was extremely nurturing and diplomatic with the kids, explaining that, "We are to make a joyful noise unto the Lord. As long as we sing with joy in our hearts, it will sound beautiful to him."

What the Lord may find joyful, human ears can find barely tolerable. Marlene mistook Mrs. Young's sweet word of encouragement as confirmation she was really doing a good job of singing her solo. On the night of the Christmas play, Marlene belted out "Silent Night." The week before, she had watched her cousin Amy compete in the Miss Coleman Yuletide Christmas Pageant. While watching the talent portion of the contest, Marlene noticed all of the girls who sang did things throughout their performances to make it more visually dramatic. Marlene decided she would add some motions and facial expressions to her performance.

Marlene sang her little heart out. She sang with power and emotion. She began the song in a soft, whispery voice with her head cast slightly downward. When she got to "All is calm, all is bright," Marlene quickly lifted her chin, widened her eyes and gracefully swept her right hand up towards the ceiling. While she was singing, she did not dare look directly at anybody in the audience. That was what her cousin advised she do to avoid stage fright. "Marlene, if you start looking at people in the audience, it will mess you up every time. Look up over their heads. If there is a church balcony, look at the railing on the balcony."

It was not until her song was finished that Marlene dared to look at the audience. She was expecting a big reaction to her riveting performance. Even she was surprised by the amount of applause she received. What surprised Marlene even more was seeing Zane Turner wiping his eyes with his handkerchief. Marlene could not believe it. She had brought big Zane Turner to tears! Next to Zane, his wife had her head down. And her shoulders were shaking. To Marlene, it looked as though she was crying hysterically.

In Marlene's little eight-year-old mind, she was convinced she had rocked the audience to their emotional core. Although Dorothy had stepped up to take the microphone for her solo,

Marlene refused to move out of her way. She wanted more time to bask in the imagined glory. As she stood there smiling, yet trying to look humble, Marlene continued to span the audience to see their reactions. The more she scanned, the more she realized the applause was them being polite. The tears and trembling shoulders were from stifled laughter. Those in the audience had enjoyed Marlene's cute and precocious on-stage antics, not her singing voice.

Back at home that night, Marlene and her folks watched the videotape her dad recorded. Marlene was inconsolable after watching that tape. "You were the hit of the show," her mom kept telling her. Marlene's mother was correct. She was the hit of the show. Everyone was rolling with laughter over the way she delivered her performance. It was all anybody at church talked about for weeks.

From that moment on, Marlene vowed to never sing in public. Nobody ever heard her sing again. At church, she opened her hymnal and moved her mouth. Her lips moved, but nothing came out. The only time she ever sang out loud was when she was sure nobody else could hear.

So, there she stood, on stage in front of twenty-some strangers with a microphone being shoved in her face. Marlene was suddenly facing her greatest phobia. The audience was clapping and cheering. *Pretty soon they'll be laughing at me*, Marlene thought to herself.

The musician began playing Jimmy Buffet's "Volcano." As his fingers started strumming the guitar, he said, "Okay ladies, I know you know this one."

Next to Marlene, Dorothy was smiling as she swayed back and forth to the music. Dorothy had no worries. Her voice was pretty good. Just as the musical intro was winding down to its last two eight counts Marlene spotted and older gentleman sitting alone at a table. He was clapping and cheering louder than anyone else in the crowd.

When she looked in his direction, his eyes locked with hers. Marlene doubted he noticed the fear in her eyes. From the way he was looking her up and down, he seemed to think she was hot.

Marlene could see from several feet away he was about two drinks past drunk and about two sips shy of passing out. His table was full of bottles and cups he had emptied throughout the night. As long as he could get up and walk, she planned to lure him up on stage.

Marlene knew it was wrong to flirt with the inebriated man, but he was the only person she thought could get her out of her predicament. Marlene knew if she could get him up on stage, he would overshadow anything she would be doing or singing.

She was sure Mark would not mind her flirting to get out of singing in public. Her husband heard her sing once when he got home earlier than expected from playing golf one Sunday afternoon. Marlene was singing *Itsy, Bitsy Spider* to Alex. Since Alex thought her singing was funny, Marlene was belting it out in a loud, screeching, operatic style. Mark was in the house a good five minutes without Marlene knowing. All the while, she was singing at the top of her lungs. After *Itsy, Bitsy Spider*, Marlene forced a couple of more tunes out her pipes. The lullabies were just a vocal warm-up. The finale was a rousing and raucous rendition of Aretha Franklin's *Respect*.

When Marlene turned around to find Mark standing there, she nearly jumped out of her skin. "Oh, I didn't realize you were home. How much of my concert did you get to enjoy?" she asked.

"I've been in the house for a few minutes," he answered.

"Well, I guess you heard enough to understand why I never sing in the car, in the shower or any other time you might hear me," she said.

Mark broke into a smile. "I thought you sounded cute. Alex loves *The Muppets*."

"I wasn't trying to sing like a MUPPET," she said. "That's my singing voice."

Mark's expression was vacillating between mortification and amusement. "Oh, well I guess I do understand why you don't sing in front of me."

They had a good laugh but agreed that Marlene's singing voice was pretty terrible. Mark thought nearly everything his wife did was terrific and sexy, except for her singing. He would surely rather her flirt with another man than to sing in public.

Giving her best come-hither look, Marlene motioned for the drunken man come onto the stage. He anxiously, but clumsily made his way up to them about the time the first vocals of the song were uttered. He was loud, stupid and completely hilarious. He created such a scene that Marlene could have left the stage, and nobody would have noticed.

Once the song was over, the singer thanked Marlene, Dorothy and the inebriated man. Marlene and Dorothy exited the stage. The drunken man hung in there for the next song. That was a relief to Marlene, who was afraid he might try and hang out with her and Dorothy. Their pizza was ready shortly after, so they grabbed it and began taking it back towards their condo before the man could have a chance to find them.

Dorothy was still laughing over the whole thing. "How fun was that?" she asked.

"Fun? I was terrified!" cried Marlene.

"Oh, I forgot about how scared you are to sing in front of people. Well, that man who came up on stage with us was so goofy that nobody paid attention to us. We could have flashed the audience, and nobody would have noticed."

"Dorothy, I sort of flirted with him to get him up there with us," Marlene admitted. "Am I terrible? I know Mark would not mind. He knows how scared I am to sing in public."

"Oh Marlene, you don't even need to worry about what people think," said Dorothy. "You're so charming and pretty. You could have gotten up there and made a fool out of yourself, and you would still have not looked silly."

"Thank you Dorothy. You are sweet, but you haven't heard me sing," said Marlene.

"Oh yes I have! Remember, I was there when you sang at church when we were little."

"That's right. You and Allison were both there. Is there not one embarrassing moment of my life the two of you haven't witnessed?"

"No, really I don't think there is. We've been through it all," said Dorothy.

Marlene nodded in agreement. "Yes Dorothy, we have. We sure have!"

Chapter 11

On their first morning at the beach, all the ladies were wide awake by 7 a.m. It would take them a couple more mornings to undo the habits of their daily schedules and reset their clocks to beach time.

As the first one up, Dorothy took a short walk by herself. She took a path that led her around the Sea Pines section of Hilton Head. Normally, Dorothy liked to wear her MP3 player and listen to music while she walked. That morning, she opted to forgo the music so she could just be with her thoughts. Dorothy wanted to soak up the feeling of being grateful for her life and the opportunity to be where she was. While she walked, she prayed. Dorothy and God had always been close; but her journey through the world of breast cancer strengthened her faith. As she walked Dorothy thanked God she was there with her friends and not in a hospital or a grave.

Once Dorothy was back from her walk, she started a pot of coffee. A few minutes later, Allison came shuffling into the kitchen. The coffee smelled so good that Allison decided to postpone her morning jog for some coffee time with Dorothy. After the coffee was brewed, they went outside to enjoy their morning java with an ocean view.

Allison wished she could snap out of her ugly bad mood and into a light, happy vacation vibe. She felt like a black cloud hanging over her friends' beach trip. "I'm sorry that I've been such a sad sack to be around lately," she said.

Dorothy felt like it was time to have a heart-to-heart with Allison. "I feel the need to break a pact I made with myself the night before we left for this trip. The pact was that I would not be overbearing, overly controlling and over-mothering to my friends. You do have complete freedom to yell at me and tell me to "shut up" if you don't want to hear this," she said.

Allison really did want to hear what Dorothy had to say. "I won't shut you up. I've been grasping at straws trying to figure out what I should do. Any advice will be welcomed."

"Sweetheart, your personality is so out-of-sync with Gary's right now," said Dorothy. "To me you have always been the perfect cheerleader. You're no longer breaking out the pom-poms and back handsprings like you did in high school. Now it's the positive words or the perfect little greeting card. You know how to make people feel better. That is your gift. It's what makes you who you are. When I think of Allison, I think of happiness and sunshine. To be any other way is just not you."

Dorothy knew much of Gary's problem stemmed from a huge well of guilt. Mitch had lost his life serving in a war. He had served his country, just like nearly every other male in the family. Gary still felt guilty he had not joined the military. "Allison, do you think Gary would feel even guiltier than he already does if he were to start moving on with his life?" asked Dorothy.

Allison knew Dorothy had a point. "I think that's the biggest part of it," said Allison. What I wish is that he would begin to feel guilty over the way he's practically abandoned me and the kids. The last thing I should do is lay another guilt trip on him, but that's just about where I'm headed. Gary was the best brother he could be to Mitch, and he still honors his memory every day. He seems to forget he also made a promise to honor me. I'm the wife that's alive and kicking. Gary barely acknowledges me anymore because he's always thinking about what he can do to honor someone who is gone."

As Dorothy and Allison were finishing their heartfelt talk, Marlene came out to the patio with her coffee. Marlene offered a bit of what she had been thinking for some time. "Allison, I wonder if Gary might consider talking to Pastor Evans or going to a counselor. I think his grief and depression is beyond what you can ever fix," she said.

Allison toyed with the same thought for some time but wondered if Gary would go for it. "I would love it if he would at least try counseling. Sometimes I'm afraid he's gotten so comfortable being sad that he's forgotten how to be happy. I don't even know if he wants to get any better. It might be easier for him to be like he is because he can cut himself out of all the family stuff without any repercussions. He's using his grief as a "Get out of Jail Free" card. There are no expectations put upon him except showing up to his job. Other than that, he can sit in the basement all he wants while I try and keep our kids' lives what they were before Mitch died."

Chapter 12

Charity could not believe how much she missed Marlene, Allison and Dorothy. She called them her three fairy godmothers. They were a lifeline for her in times of trouble. The bond she had with them was real, strong as steel and had been built through adversity.

Although she had her three fairy godmothers, Charity's life was not a fairytale, and her ex-husband was certainly no Prince Charming. Shortly after Charity had their baby girl, he cheated on her with a lady old enough to be Charity's evil stepmother. To make matters worse, his mistress was no other than the hairdresser and trusted good friend of Marlene, Dorothy and Allison.

When the affair was first discovered, Charity thought of moving back to West Virginia to be with her parents. She could not imagine there was any other way she would be able to manage working and raising her daughter, Blaney. She knew her ex-husband, Joe was not going to be much help as a co-parent. He was immature and impulsive. Joe could be a great dad one week and a sorry parent the next. Charity feared she would not be able to single-handedly cover for all of Joe's parental shortcomings. Charity was right in one respect. She could not do it all herself without going insane. The task of raising her daughter while working full-time was overwhelming. Sometimes, it was more than she could handle on her own. Whenever Charity thought she could not manage her life as a single mom, her friends stepped up.

It took them all three leaving to make Charity realize what a big part of her life they had become. Charity asked their advice on everything from parenting to fashion. With them gone, she felt a distinct absence of support.

When Charity got married and left West Virginia, she was only twenty-three. At the time, she felt like such a grownup. It took having a child and going through a divorce to make her realize she still had lots of growing up to do. Marlene, Allison and Dorothy were helping Allison learn to be a better mom and a stronger, more mature woman.

Charity could not believe a day after her friends had all taken off for the beach, she was in need of womanly advice. For the first time in her life, Charity had two men pulling at her heart strings. It was making her lose sleep at night. If she did not get some advice quickly, she was going to go nuts.

Charity decided to leave a message on Marlene's cell phone. "Hey Marlene, hope you ladies are having the best time," she said. "If you get a chance, give me a call sometime. It's nothing about the shop. Everything's running smooth as can be. It's about men. Don't worry, not about any of your men. I've got a new situation on my hands."

Charity hoped she was not being like a pesky kid sister by calling her friends while they were on vacation. If she thought it could wait, she would have talked to them when they got home from their trip. Timing was the problem. Marlene, Dorothy and Allison would not be getting back to Coleman until the day after Charity was planning to leave for West Virginia.

* * *

Later that night, Marlene returned Charity's call. "Okay girl, give us the dirt. What's Joe done this time? " she asked.

It was fair to assume Joe was the problem. He usually was. "No, it's not Joe this time," said Charity. Why don't you go ahead and put me on speaker phone? That way, you won't have to repeat my whole story. Plus, I might need everyone's input on this one."

Once she was on speaker phone, Charity greeted everyone. They chit-chatted about how things were at the beach, and then Charity began her story. "In high school, I was madly in love with this guy named Rick. We never really dated, but there was always a little bit of a spark between us. Secretly, I swore to myself that Rick was my future husband. Rick and I sort of lost touch for a few years when he went off to college. Then, about two years after we graduated from high school, he called me out of the blue. We started talking every few days and talked about hanging out whenever he came back into town to visit his parents. Right before Rick was supposed to come back into town, I met Joe. Of course, I have to wonder if my life might be different now if I had spent time with Rick instead of Joe. Last month, Rick found me on Facebook. He sent me a message just to ask how I was doing. Then last week, Rick said he wants to meet up for coffee next weekend when I go to West Virginia to visit my parents. I'm excited that I'm going to see Rick, but I feel guilty. Should I tell Clay about this?"

Dorothy was always the best in the group to deliver sound advice. "Charity, nothing has happened. If you feel the need to tell him you're going to have coffee with an old friend, that's fine. I don't think there's any use telling him anything more," she advised.

Allison added her thoughts. "Charity, haven't you told Clay several times you aren't ready for a relationship? Even if something does happen, it's not like you'll be cheating. Clay cares more for you right now than you care for him, and he knows it. It might hurt him if you go out with another man, but he cannot claim you've led him on."

Marlene pointed to the technicalities of a date versus meeting a friend. "I think coffee qualifies as a strictly friends thing," she said. It's less than dinner, but more than keeping touch over the internet or phone. Nothing is going to happen. Coffee's just coffee. Have you ever heard of any couple getting it on after a strong cup of coffee? It's completely innocent. He might as well be asking you to church."

They were all of the opinion going to coffee with Rick would be no big deal. Charity hated she felt conflicted. She was normally a decisive person. Men were the only thing that could make her wishy-washy.

When Charity divorced Joe, she swore she would wait one year before accepting a date with any man. She broke that rule by an invitation to spend New Year's Eve with Clay. It was not easy to turn down Clay Baines. He was estimated by many ladies to be one of the hottest men in Southwest Virginia, a fact that had been validated when a local magazine featured him in their yearly "Southwest Virginia's Most Beautiful Singles" edition. Ever since that piece came out in the magazine with Clay pictured in Wranglers, an International Harvester T-shirt and baseball cap, women all around Southwest Virginia called him the "Sexy Farmer."

For the women who got past the photo and read the article about Clay, the admiration was deeper than a physical attraction. The article described a man who was tough and hardworking yet thoughtful and sensitive. Clay had a deep, almost poetic love for the land his family farmed for generations. The article quoted him as saying, "This land, the crops and the animals aren't just a job to me. I love the fact that my hard work sustains life. If I don't give it my all, the crops will wither and the animals will starve. I see relationships as being the same way. You can't neglect love and then expect it to grow and flourish."

Clay had shown Charity he was not just good with words. His actions were true to the way he portrayed himself in the article. He was a perfect gentleman in every way. Clay was ten times better to Charity than Joe had ever been. If Clay were not so nice, Charity would not be worried about meeting Rick. In the back of her mind, Charity thought maybe something could happen with Rick. Maybe that torch she carried all through high school would still be flickering.

Before Charity got off the phone, she updated her friends on the Hens latest stab at their character. "The Hens are still talking about how terrible they think you gals are for going off, footloose and fancy free to the beach,"said Charity. "They've come up with a new nickname for you three."

Marlene could only imagine what the new nickname might be. In the past, the Hens had referred to her as "skanky pie," "snooty pie," "ho-berry pie," and "slutty turnover" among other things. "I'm sure it involves a combination of some reference to us being of questionable virtue, plus something to do with some sort of pie," said Marlene.

Charity laughed, "Oh, you know those ladies well. You all have been nicknamed the Sand Tarts."

Marlene, Charity and Dorothy all got a kick out of Charity's announcement. Allison needed the cheering up. "I think we ought to start calling ourselves the Sand Tarts. The Hens meant it as an insult, but I think it's kind of cute," she said.

Dorothy shared Allison's opinion regarding the new moniker. "The nickname's kind of cute, and we're kind of cute, so let's be the Sand Tarts."

Chapter 13

Dorothy had not had on a bathing suit since before her whole cancer ordeal had begun. She never felt very confident about her body. Dorothy had never been really overweight, but she had never exactly been svelte either. There was a stubborn ten pounds she was perpetually battling. All her life, Dorothy hated putting on a bathing suit. It was strange, but she no longer felt as anxious about her figure. Before, she might have been intimidated by Marlene's long legs and curves or Allison's petite frame. Coming through cancer had given Dorothy a deeper appreciation for many things, including her body. She never had and never would look like a swimsuit model, but Dorothy was blessed to have survived cancer and welcomed the opportunity to put on her bathing suit and enjoy time with her friends on the beach.

Thanks to some new healthy habits, Dorothy actually looked really good. After she got her clean bill of health, she decided to become very proactive in taking care of herself. She began working out every day and cleaned up her eating habits. Dorothy traded her potato chips and cookies for carrot sticks and fresh fruit. She was not a complete health nut. A cheeseburger, some pizza or a piece of cake sometimes made their way to Dorothy's plate, but she became much more aware of what she was putting into her body.

There were days when Dorothy could feel the toll the cancer and its treatments took on her system. Seeing that last drop of chemotherapy go into her veins did not mean the effects of those chemo drugs were over. Some days, Dorothy felt a sense of fatigue that made her want to stay on the couch, covered in a blanket watching television all day.

Her mind had to overpower her body on those days. Dorothy would tell herself, "All during my treatments, I just wanted my life to be normal again. Normal means going to work and taking care of my daughter, not staying home on the couch all day by myself while other people do my job and take care of my kid."

Somehow, she managed to push through the fatigue and go on with her day. Dorothy's mind was good at overpowering her body, but it was not good at remembering things. Her mom had warned her about "chemobrain." Dorothy's mom said, "Sweetheart, for about a year after my treatments ended, I could not remember a thing. One time I walked out of the grocery store without my groceries. Another time, I walked down to the mailbox to put a letter in. When I got back to the house, that letter was still in my hand. There was a fog filling my head where my brain used to be."

The forgetfulness and inability to focus bothered Dorothy the most. All of her life, she had prided herself on having superb organizational skills. A series of lists and other specific reminders helped, but she was just not as sharp as she used to be.

Marlene, who was a scatterbrain, joked that Dorothy had joined her world. "Dorothy, even with 'chemobrain,' I think you've got it more together than I do."

Dorothy knew her fatigue and memory would improve with time. She might never be completely the same way as before, but for the time being, she was alive and felt like she had won the battle of all battles. Instead of focusing on what she had lost, Dorothy celebrated positive changes she had made in her life.

All of the working out and healthy eating were beginning to show. Her legs were thinner and her arms were cut with muscle. Her skin that had become so sallow and dry during her chemotherapy treatments was regaining its radiance. Erica Flynn, Coleman's resident Mary Kay guru, had been Dorothy's consultant on all things skin and cosmetics for many years. Erica had babied Dorothy's skin through all of the chemo and hormonal shifts. She was constantly treating Dorothy to facials and free make-up applications to boost her spirits. Once all of the treatments had been completed, Erica's expertise helped Dorothy find a natural but slightly more daring make-up look that made her blue eyes pop.

Rhonda was Dorothy's hairstylist and had been just as helpful with all of Dorothy's follicle problems as Erica had been with her skin and make-up. When Dorothy began losing her hair, Rhonda styled her wigs. The wigs looked so good that when Dorothy was out, women would come up to her to ask who did her cut and color.

Recently, Dorothy's locks had begun to grow back into a crown of short curls Dorothy dyed platinum blond, which made her blue eyes pop. Tom, Dorothy's husband always thought he liked long hair on women until he saw Dorothy's short blond do. "Edgy and hot" is how he described Dorothy's short blond hair. He liked it so much that when Rhonda offered to do hair extensions for free, Tom told Dorothy he thought he liked it much better like it was. Who knew chemo would help Dorothy find a new look her husband would love?

Dorothy also developed a new sense of style. For her whole life, She had been in the matchy matchy clothing club. Most of her outfits could have been described as "Garanimals for Grownups." The pants or skirts and the tops were bought in sets and usually were adorned with cutesy appliqués and embroidery. It was Dorothy's way of putting together outfits. "If I buy things that the store has put together, at least I know that I match," she said.

It was an easy yet unimaginative and predictable way to get dressed. Dorothy knew her style was boring, but she did not have the confidence to dress any other way.

When Dorothy began wearing her new short hairstyle, her old clothes no longer looked right. Cool hair required cool outfits. With Marlene's help, Dorothy began shopping online for hipper, more flattering clothes to replace her old wardrobe.

It was not just the outside that had changed. Dorothy was emotionally and spiritually so much stronger than she had been before the cancer. It was impossible to go through such a thing and not be changed.

Every day, Dorothy had to make a conscious decision not to focus on her fears. Remission did not mean cancer would not ever stake its claim on her again. She kept hearing and reading about the five-year-cancer-free benchmark. That marked a point at which a cancer survivor was less likely to suffer a recurrence of the disease.

Dorothy refused to give much thought to the five year mark. Each day was a gift, whether she had one day, five years or fifty years. Cancer might strike her again, but so might a freight train. Nobody was guaranteed one more minute of life. Dorothy would be paralyzed by fear if she spent much time thinking about the fact her cancer could come back. She had decided she would live each day with gratitude. She was thankful for her life. During her darkest, worst times of fighting cancer, she never dreamed she would soon be at the beach with her girlfriends. Dorothy was going to celebrate the day by putting on her cute new bathing suit and having a blast!

The bathing suits she brought on the trip reflected her new fashion-forward style. That morning, she chose to wear a hot pink and Kelly green Ralph Lauren Polo tankini. As her cover-up, she wore a hot pink terry cloth short skirt with a drawstring closure. A hot pink visor, some big tortoiseshell sunglasses and pink flip-flops completed her look. All the hot pink proved she could never completely get away from being matchy matchy, but it was definitely put together in a more interesting way.

Marlene and Allison were quick to compliment Dorothy when she took off her cover-up out on the beach that day. Dorothy always felt self-conscious to be in a swimsuit around her two best buddies. Marlene had the curves of a 1940s pinup girl and Allison had the petite body of a teenager.

Since she had began working out so much, Dorothy did not feel like the frumpy one of the bunch. Her body looked strong and athletic. Even if she did not look so good, Dorothy would have been thankful to simply be alive. Looking good despite all of the wear and tear on her body was a bonus.

Dorothy's confidence may have made her just a little cocky. When some younger guys walked by on the beach and whistled, she looked up from her magazine and smiled at them. Boy, did she feel stupid when she saw the men walk up to a couple of twenty-somethings in string bikinis that were lying in the sun just a few feet from Dorothy. So, maybe those young men were not whistling at her, but Dorothy knew that, to the one man that mattered, her husband Tom, she looked perfect. Tom always told his wife that he thought she was beautiful. Finally, she believed him.

Dorothy looked to see if either of her friends saw her mistakenly smile at the men she thought had whistled at her. Marlene and Allison would have found it humorous, possibly not letting her live it down for the whole trip.

Marlene had fallen asleep while reading a book. Allison was awake but had not been paying attention to what had happened with Dorothy and the whistling boys. Behind her sunglasses, Allison's eyes were deeply fixated on a family that was playing on the beach. It was a mom and dad with their two kids. The children looked to be about the same ages as Allison's kids. They were tossing a Frisbee back and forth to each other, all the while talking and laughing. They reminded Allison of a family she used to know: her own.

Down the beach a ways, there was a mom picking up shells with her two kids. No dad was in sight. Sadly, that reminded Allison of her current situation. The biggest difference between the two families on the beach was the absence of a dad. Both families were smiling and laughing.

In the last few weeks, Allison had been noticing lots of families headed by single moms that were doing just fine. Even with all they had been through, Mitch's widow and their kids were doing reasonably well. She had to wonder if she and her kids would be happier making a life that did not have to be so accommodating of Gary's woeful moods. If living with Gary was no longer the best thing for her children, Allison had to consider a different living situation.

Chapter 14

It had been two nights since Monique had put the mysterious package in a hole in the woods. Burying it had not given her mind any peace at all.

She had taken to Googling herself obsessively. She was afraid whatever was on the videotape might also turn up on the Internet. It was possible the package was only the first component in a series of secrets.

Monique tried to go back in her mind to see if she could recall a particular person from her past who might want to cause problems for her. The going back was painful for her. When Monique changed her life, she put those times behind her. Trying to pull them up in her memory was like taking a giant step backwards.

What made Monique feel like she had gone completely macabre and out of her mind was her compulsion to keep going back to the spot in the woods were she buried the tape. It was like a criminal who kept going back to the crime scene. Monique felt like she had to reassure herself the package was still in the ground. Last time she checked, she could have sworn that rock looked like it had been moved a couple of inches.

That morning, Monique prayed and prayed about her situation. She remembered a verse she had been taught as a youngster in Vacation Bible School. It was from the book of I Peter. Tears came to her eyes as she recited the words " . . . at the present, you may be temporarily harassed by all kinds of trials. This is no accident — it happens to prove your faith . . . "

Monique quickly realized the irony of turning to God when she had been keeping a truth from her husband. How could she ask for Christ's guidance when she was being dishonest to Bo? It was decided. She would tell Bo about the tape as soon as he got home from the farm that evening.

Monique had been a lot of things in her life, but she had never been a phony. Fakery was something she truly despised. Her grandmother's favorite saying was, "If you're not real, you're not nothin'."

One of the things Bo loved so much about her was how genuine and completely honest she was. Monique knew Bo would be forgiving about the tape no matter what was on it. What he might not get over was the fact that she had been deceitful by not telling him about it.

Monique realized most men would not be forgiving of a past as colorful as hers. She worried seeds of doubt might be planted in Bo's mind when he found out she kept a secret from him. If those seeds were planted, Monique feared they would bear weeds; weeds that would randomly pop up like stray dandelions on a well-manicured lawn. Monique had seen it happen in other people's relationships. A lack of trust could become a pervasive force that would forever linger over a marriage.

Ever since the tape had arrived, Monique tried to think of some way to justify not telling Bo. When all avenues had been considered, she knew the only right thing to do was tell him. She was sick of worrying about it. If the timing was not so horrible, she would have left work and driven over to the farm and told Bo right then.

However, it was not something to be done while he was working. In the privacy and comfort of their own home, Monique would sit him down and come out with it. Her suggestion would be to destroy the tape and never give it another thought. If Bo would agree to that suggestion, it would all be over and done.

Chapter 15

On the third day, the ladies decided to head over to Savannah, Georgia, the home of Marlene's idol, Paula Deen. Marlene was a woman who would prefer to meet Paula Deen over Brad Pitt, showing a good recipe for gooey butter cake was more appealing to her than a fine specimen of movie star beefcake.

Marlene knew that her dream encounter with Paula Deen in Savannah was not likely to happen. "I've looked at her website recently. I happen to know she will be traveling a lot this month. Then, there's the restaurant, the magazine and spending time with her grandson, Jack."

Allison always got so amused when she heard Marlene talk about Paula Deen. "You know way too much about her. It's an obsession with you. You talk about her and her family like you're acquainted."

Marlene did not argue with Allison. "Yes, I am a tad bit obsessed,"she admitted. "If I were totally obsessed, I would have insisted on leaving early this morning to get a seat for lunch at Lady and Sons. I might have even reserved three spots on the Paula Deen Cruise that departs from here and floats over to Savannah if it weren't for our excursion clause. Don't you think I didn't consider getting up before you and Allison and sneaking out to Savannah before you all would know I was gone? But that would be breaking the excursion clause."

The excursion clause was a verbal agreement amongst the women. It was a clause that was drawn up in the car on their way to Hilton Head. Allison initiated the discussion that led to the clause. "I'm going to go ahead and tell you ladies now. Since I'm in such desperate need of some relaxation, I plan to not do a whole lot on this trip," she said. "I know you guys might want to do some shopping and day trips, but I don't see me doing much besides lying on the beach and eating some good meals."

Dorothy thought Allison might have a really good idea. "I can remember doing vacations when I was little, where we ran ourselves to death," she said. "We tried to see every attraction, amusement park and museum. We'd come home from those trips more tired than we had been before we left home. I don't want to do that on this trip. Let's go back feeling rested and restored instead of running ourselves ragged."

Marlene was more hesitant about agreeing with Allison. "Sounds good to me, except for going to Savannah. If you girls don't want to go, I understand. I don't care to go by myself."

Allison and Dorothy kind of wanted to see Savannah also but did not want it to become a scheduled, stressful thing. Marlene reached a compromise with her friends, and the excursion clause was hatched. The clause stated that excursions would not involve taking a tour, having to set an alarm to get up early or looking at real estate in exchange for putt-putt vouchers.

The ladies arrived in Savannah by lunch time. They decided to eat at a cute little seafood restaurant. They were seated outside in a beautiful little garden full of flowers. Their table was white painted wrought iron with a colorful striped cotton tablecloth. A nearby tree had bottles made of all different colors of glass hanging from its branches.

At some point during the time they were discussing what they planned to order, Marlene went silent, then gasped, "Oh my gosh, y'all. I think that's her!"

Allison and Dorothy turned to see who Marlene was talking about. "No, don't look. She'll know I'm talking about her," hissed Marlene.

Allison and Dorothy snapped back around as per Marlene's instructions, although Dorothy really did not see the point. "Everyone's staring. Don't you think she's used to it by now?" asked Dorothy.

Marlene's excitement was growing by the millisecond. "So you think it's really her?" she squealed.

Dorothy took another look. "I'm pretty sure; like ninety-nine percent."

Allison urged Marlene to find out. "Why don't you go talk to her? Say, 'Hey, are you Paula Deen?'"

"I don't know if I can to that. I mean she's here to have lunch. She might think I'm rude if I just go over there," said Marlene.

Dorothy wanted Marlene to seize the opportunity. "Marlene, when will you ever again have the chance to meet Paula Deen?" she asked.

Marlene was trying to think of a way to meet Paula without actually going over to her table and intruding on her lunch. Paula was sitting with a group of women. Nobody was taking notes. There were no laptops. They were all dressed very casually, meaning it probably was not a business meeting. Marlene did not spot Paula's daughter-in-law Brooke or niece Corrie, so she assumed it was not a family get-together. Marlene figured that it was a leisurely lunch with girlfriends. It would not be too terribly rude of her to go over and interrupt, but she could not bring herself to do it.

"Okay you two, help me think of a way to talk to her without being obvious," she said.

Allison was quick to come up with a sneaky scheme. "Okay, you know that last picture you had made of Alex?" she asked.

Marlene was anxious to hear where Allison's plan was going. "Yes, the one where Tom came out to the house and took a picture of him wearing overalls in his red wagon. That picture could be an ad for Gap, it's so cute."

Dorothy guessed where Allison's plan was going. "Oh, Paula loves kids, doesn't she?" asked Dorothy.

Marlene knew for a fact Paula Deen adored children. "She wanted grandkids so bad she couldn't stand it. Now, that little grandson, Jack, is the light of her life. I wish Alex was with me right now. She'd go nuts over him."

Allison's plan was the next best thing to having Alex there in the flesh. "So, you're totally going to use your cute little boy to meet Paula. I know you ordered a bunch of copies of that photo, so if you lose one, it's not too big of a deal. If this works, you won't lose anything and you'll get to meet her. I know you have at least one of those photos in your pocketbook."

Once Marlene decided Allison's plan was so silly that it might work, she was too nervous to eat her lunch. "Okay, girls. I'm going to do it. I feel like a big dork, but I'm going to do it."

Dorothy pointed out the correlations between that moment and their first night of vacation. "This is just like the singing. You were so afraid of making a fool of yourself. That didn't really matter, but this does. You'll be kicking yourself if you don't go talk to Paula. Get your butt up and go over there!" she urged.

Marlene scraped up every bit of courage she had, and walked towards Paula's table. She already had Alex's picture in the pocket of her shorts so that she could drop it. Hopefully Paula wouldn't become wise to her trickery.

Marlene wondered if her nerves might get the best of her as she approached the table where Paula Deen was engaged in an animated conversation with that unmistakable Deep South molasses twang. Her hands moved as she talked, making the diamonds on her fingers flicker in the faint streams of sunlight that peaked in through the trees.

When she had decided that it was time to carry out her plan, Marlene discreetly reached into her pocket to grab Alex's photo. A feeling of guilt rushed through her as she was about to drop the photo on the floor. *It's so pathetic that I'm using my cute son to meet a celebrity* she thought to herself.

Marlene lurked so closed to Paula's seat she could smell her perfume. It was time to drop the photo and go to the restroom. Allison told her to act like she was looking for something on the way back from the restroom. Hopefully, someone from Paula's table would notice her and ask if she needed help. Then, Marlene would find the photo in the floor right behind Paula's table.

The plan would never go that far. Paula Deen must have felt the presence of an obsessed fan behind her because she turned around in her seat. The brilliant twinkle in her blue eyes and the big, approachable smile made Marlene feel like Paula might be up for a bit of conversation.

"I am so sorry to interrupt your lunch, but I had to come over to say "Hi" and tell you how much you have inspired me," gushed Marlene.

Marlene knew she had not said anything original. Paula Deen probably had about one hundred people a day tell her the exact same thing. To Marlene's surprise, Paula acted as if that was the first time anyone had ever come up to pay her a compliment. "Honey, you are so sweet. Thank you so much! " beamed Paula Deen.

Marlene could not believe Paula spoke to her. She felt pressure to think of something clever to say back and turn the encounter into an actual conversation. "Paula, I know you're eating lunch with your friends, and it's probably such a pain when people ask for autographs during your personal time, but it would mean so much to me if I could get your autograph," said Marlene sweetely.

Paula Deen proved to be as gracious as she seemed on television. Without hesitation she reached into her pocketbook for a pen and was ready to give Marlene her autograph. In her haste to ambush Paula, Marlene had left her purse sitting on the table. The only thing she had with her was Alex's photo. "Um, would you mind to sign the back of my son's picture? I don't have anything else with me for you to sign. My little boy knows who you are because I watch you on TV so much. It will thrill his little heart to death if you sign the back of his picture."

Marlene found the key to opening the door to a having full-blown conversation with Miss Paula Deen, the queen of southern cooking. Marlene's picture reminded Paula of her grandson Jack. They talked about Jack and Alex for a good five minutes.

Marlene wound up telling Paula about Cutie Pies and how she started by making pies with her grandmother. Paula even gave her the name and address of one of her people, telling Marlene, "Now you send me one of your best pie recipes and a story about your business. I'll try and make one of your pies on my show."

Marlene and Paula talked for a few more minutes. Before Paula left the restaurant, Marlene got her BlackBerry so Dorothy could take a photo of the two.

Marlene could have gone back to Coleman at that very moment. Her vacation had already exceeded all of her expectations. Talking to Paula meant Marlene's whole LIFE had exceeded expectations. Paula Deen was everything Marlene had dreamed she would be.

On the trip back to Hilton Head from Savannah, Marlene sent a picture from her BlackBerry to everyone back home. It was of her and Paula posed cheek-to-cheek, just like old girlfriends.

Allison could not help but feel somewhat responsible for Marlene's chance meeting with Paula Deen. "Let us not forget that if it were not for the excursion clause, we would have been at Lady and Son or on a Paula Deen Cruise instead of in that restaurant," she reminded Marlene.

"Yes, Allison, you are right. If it had not been for the excursion clause, I would have never met Paula Deen."

Chapter 16

The ladies decided to spend some time at Harbour Town, a development located just a few minutes from their condo that included lots of shops and restaurants. As implied by the name, Harbour Town was built around a harbor. The harbor's marina was filled with beautiful boats from all over the country. There were boats of all sizes, from old wooden boats polished to a shine to luxury yachts that were large enough for a family to live on for the summer.

What made Harbour Town most famous was its iconic light-house. The lighthouse was located right at the eighteenth hole of the golf course, which was a regular stop on the PGA tour.

Dorothy got the idea to rent bikes for the day to ride over to Harbour Town. "It will be fun and some good exercise. If Hilton Head's anything, it is bike friendly. There are bike paths all over the place. I feel like we'll be missing out on the whole Hilton Head experience if we don't ride bikes somewhere," she asked.

Marlene and Allison were game for the bike ride. Once they had eaten breakfast and gotten dressed, they all walked across the street to a place that rented bicycles. They took off on their bikes, guided by the Harbour Town Lighthouse in the distance.

Dorothy took a few Zumba classes to get in shape for her beach trip. She told the ladies what her Zumba teacher had shared regarding endurance and overexertion. "If you can comfortably speak while working out, then you're okay. Being so out of breath that you can't even say your name means you need to slow it down a little."

The ladies put Dorothy's talk test through its paces. They chatted comfortably all the way to Harbour Town, making them each feel like they must have been in pretty good shape.

Dorothy thought the realization they were pretty fit opened the door for her to propose her idea. "Okay, here's something I think we oughta do. When I was going to Kingsport for some of my cancer treatments, I met the most inspiring lady named Deb Johnson," Dorothy explained. "Deb was a few months ahead of me in her chemo treatments. She was able to answer all of my questions and convinced me things would eventually get much better. Last year, Deb participated in the Susan G. Koman Race for the Cure in Kingsport. She said it was exhilarating to be with so many people united for one cause. There's going to be a Susan G. Komen Race for the Cure in Kingsport this coming October. Why don't we get some other women to join us and start a team? A team needs ten or more women. I can be the team captain and get it all together. We don't have to run. Our whole team can walk the race course."

Allison and Marlene loved Dorothy's idea to participate as a team in the Susan G. Komen Race for the Cure. Later, while they lunched on crab cakes at Crazy Crab, Marlene shared what was on her mind. "I have the perfect name for our team. We can be the Sand Tarts!"

Chapter 17

When Charity first moved to Coleman, Charlotte Holt was one of the last people she ever thought would be her friend. Charlotte had been a Hen for many years. Since her mom had been a Hen, Charlotte was welcomed into the flock as a teenager.

All the Hens tended to be heavy-handed in their attacks on Marlene, but Charlotte was particularly evil when Marlene was the target. It was all due to Glen Davis.

Charlotte spent most of her life pining for Glen Davis. Glen had spent almost as much time pining for an uninterested Marlene. Charlotte's insane romantic jealousy drove her to say some terrible things about Marlene.

Eventually, Glen and Charlotte dated. The romance that had been so built up in Charlotte's mind wound up being a giant disappointment. Glen was no prince as Charlotte had expected. He was arrogant, immature and unfaithful.

After Glen, Charlotte met a man named Chuck Weaver. Nobody would have ever put the two of them together. Charlotte was always as stuffy and tightly laced as a Victorian corset. Chuck was Grizzly Adams on a Harley. He was a big, bearded, imposing man with a heart of solid gold. They were an odd combination, but the relationship worked.

Charlotte kept the relationship a secret for some time. The Hens resorted to spying on Charlotte in attempts to find the identity of her secret boyfriend. When Charlotte found out that the Hens had been spying on her, she and her mom quit the group.

An olive branch was extended from Charlotte to Marlene soon after she quit the Hens. After Marlene's son was born, Charlotte surprised her with a handmade baby blanket and a sincere apology.

That was all it took for Marlene to forgive everything Charlotte said and did over the years. Soon Charlotte, was good friends with Marlene, Allison, Dorothy and Charity. It was Charlotte and Charity who became particularly close. During Charity's divorce, Charlotte was a huge source of support. She was one of the people with whom Charity most liked to discuss things when she needed advice.

Charity decided to see if Charlotte could meet her for lunch. She wanted to talk with Charlotte about her upcoming coffee date with Rick. "Charlotte, if you're free I'd like to have lunch tomorrow. I'd like to talk about something before I leave for West Virginia."

"I can tell by the tone of your voice something major is on your mind. I'm dying to know what's going on, but I won't even ask until we have lunch. Chuck is grilling a chicken tonight. How about I use the leftovers to make us a couple of spinach and strawberry salads with blue cheese and chicken on top?" Charlotte asked.

Charity loved that idea. "Oh, you know your grilled chicken and strawberry salad is my favorite thing in the world to eat for lunch. That sounds perfect. Why don't we meet at the park? I'll bring a jug of tea and some pie for dessert."

* * *

The unfortunate thing about new road projects in Coleman is the town would lose some really beautiful land to development. Trees would be cut down, big rock formations would be excavated and green and open fields would be leveled.

Coleman's planning commission made a very popular and wise decision when they decided to increase the size of the town's park before someone could come in to develop the land. The result of that decision was a nine-acre square of land that included a playground, jogging path, picnic area and a small amphitheatre. In the center of it all was a stone fountain dedicated to Perry Coleman, the man for whom the town was named.

Charlotte got to the park first and found them a picnic spot by the fountain. She placed a big heap of salad on each of two paper plates and laid out some napkins and plastic forks. Charity arrived a couple minutes later. She began talking before she even sat down. "Charlotte, I am not one to freak out, but I'm a little freaked out about this weekend," she said.

Charlotte was confused. "About going to West Virginia?" she asked.

"No, not going to West Virginia. It's that I've got a date in West Virginia," Charity clarified.

Charlotte really liked Clay and hoped that things would work out for him and Charity. The way Charity was talking made her think the date was not with Clay, but she hoped her inclination was wrong.

"Is Clay going up to meet your family?" she asked hopefully.

"No, it's a guy from high school. He found me on Facebook and asked me to have coffee while I'm in town," she said.

Charlotte was interested to hear Charity explain her situation, but was also concerned about Clay's feelings. "I know you're not ready to get serious with anyone, but I'd just hate to see you mess up what could be a good thing. Clay is crazy about you; I can see it in the way he looks at you," she said.

Charity and Charlotte engaged in many long talks since becoming friends. What Charlotte had concluded about Charity and men was that Charity had a penchant for choosing the wrong one. She wanted a challenge; a guy who nobody expected to settle down but who she could tame and make her own.

That was Charity's ex-husband in a nutshell. Joe was the high school football star; a hometown hero. Back when he was younger, he could have any girl in Southwest Virginia. Charity loved the fact she thought she made Joe want her and only her. A few years and a baby later, Charity discovered Joe was nowhere close to being ready to settle down.

Charlotte had some experience with finding out her knight in shining armor was nothing more than a loser wrapped in tinfoil. She chased Glen Davis for decades until Glen just gave up and asked her out. What Charlotte discovered was Glen was nothing like the man she built up in her mind for all those years.

Charlotte had to wonder if Charity built up her high school crush in the same way she built up Glen. "Charity, why do you think you and this guy never dated in high school?" asked Charlotte.

"Well, I always had a huge crush on him. We were buddies all through school, but it just never worked out that we were anything more. You know, I don't think my parents would have let me go out with him anyway," she said.

Charlotte gave a knowing grin. "And why would your parents forbid you to go out with him?" she asked.

"Mom and Dad got a little creeped out by him. Rick was polite and all, but my parents thought he was a phony. They called him a 'devil in disguise.' I guess it was because they'd hear stuff about Rick. He had this reputation of being a hard partier and a ladies' man, and he sort of was, but I could see the great guy underneath all that. Of course, I thought the same thing about Joe when I met him."

Charlotte did not want to be condescending to her friend, but she felt a need to point out a pattern. "What did your parents say about Joe when they first met him?" she asked.

"They were leery of him too" answered Charity. "Dad noticed how much Joe talked about his old days as a high school football player. He was afraid Joe was too focused on his past to be making much of a future. When he started going to school to be a welder, they were starting to become convinced he had grown up. My parents prayed Joe had grown up, but had their suspicions. When he cheated on me, their suspicions were confirmed. Guess I'm not so good at detecting a 'devil in disguise.'"

Chapter 18

"Why are vacations over so fast?" Allison asked. She could not believe they only had two days left in Hilton Head. She was excited about seeing Cicilly and Garret but could not muster up any enthusiasm about going back to Gary.

"I have had this awful thought several times over the past few days that I go and get Cicilly and Garret, bring them down here and we spend the entire summer away from home. I wonder if Gary would even notice if we left for the whole summer."

Marlene hated to think of Allison letting the last part of her vacation be ruined by apprehension over going back home. "Allison, you can't keep living like this," Marlene said. "I think Gary's too far into his own dark hole right now to see how sad you've been. You have to tell him how you feel. By letting this go on without saying anything, you're enabling him. Gary needs some intervention to get on with his life. It's probably going to be up to you to confront him."

The word "enabling" riled up something in Allison. She herself was partially responsible for her own predicament. It was time to try and change things, meaning Allison would have to be confrontational with Gary. She was going to have to change from being the encouraging cheerleader to an in-your- face drill sergeant.

* * *

That night after her friends had gone to bed, Allison grabbed her cell phone and headed out to the beach. Allison sent Gary a text so she would not wake the kids, "call me plz."

When Gary called, his voice sounded like he was a little bit glad to hear from his wife. "Hey Allison, I bet you want to talk to the kids, but they just went to bed. Do you want me to go upstairs to see if they're still awake?" he asked.

"No, Gary. I don't want you to wake them up. I talked to them this morning. I want to talk to you," she said in a serious voice.

Gary sounded puzzled. "You need to talk to me? Is something up?" he asked.

The absurdity of Gary's question annoyed Allison. "Yeah, something's up. Why wouldn't I want to talk to my husband? You act like it's strange I want to have a real conversation with you. Of course we haven't had a real conversation in quite some time," she said.

Gary could tell that Allison was crying. "Allison, why are you lashing out at me like this?" he asked. "Don't get so upset."

"Gary, I've BEEN upset," she said. "It's just now coming out. I feel like a widow. I'm practically a single parent. You have almost nothing to do with me or the kids."

Gary's tone became defensive, which was better than the dry monotone Allison was used to. "You know Mitch's death has been hard on me, and I've been so busy," he justified.

"Gary, don't blame this on being busy," she said. "I'm plenty busy myself, running the kids around to all of their activities while you barricade yourself in the basement watching television."

"Allison, do you expect me to go on like nothing has happened? he said." "You married me for better or for worse. Now, that things are not so rosy, you're no longer happy with me."

"We're supposed to go through the bad things TOGETHER. You are totally shutting me out. I married you for better or for worse assuming we'd be a team when something bad happened. I don't expect you to go on like nothing has happened, but I do expect you to go on. Mitch was taken from his family. You've taken yourself out of our lives. Does this have to become a double-tragedy?" she asked.

"Allison, this caught me off guard. I don't know what to say right now. I'll try and do better," he said.

"No Gary, that's not good enough. I don't want you to try and do better. I want you to PROMISE to do better. Don't say you'll try to come to Garret's ballgames. Show up to his ball-games. Don't tell me you'll help Cicilly with her homework if you get home from work in time. Come home, sit down at the table with your daughter and help her with her homework. If I'm going to have to raise the kids all by myself, just be straight with me right now, and tell me. I can handle that better than I can deal with this state of limbo that's been my life with you since Mitch died."

Allison had put the ball in Gary's court. If he did not plan on things changing, she was offering up an opportunity to come out with it. In a way, she was being a chicken. Allison did not want to bear the guilt of leaving Gary during his darkest moment. If it was not going to work out, it would be much easier if he was the one to call it quits.

After a period of silence that felt like hours, Gary responded. "Allison, are you thinking about leaving me?" he asked softly.

Allison's plan to have Gary be the one to talk about leaving her had been thrown back in her direction. She wanted to lie and tell Gary she was not thinking about leaving. After all, she had suddenly unloaded on him. Telling him she not only had been thinking about leaving but had planned her exit strategy would be too much for him to handle.

The truth was, Allison had been looking at the classifieds to assess the possibility of finding a nursing job. Before having kids, she worked as a nurse. She knew if she and Gary were to get a divorce, she would need to re-enter the work force on a full-time basis. Allison did not want to leave Gary, and at one time, the thought they would ever not be together was unfathomable. Gary had been Allison's buddy since they were kids and sweetheart since college. She could scarcely remember her life before him. Allison hoped Gary still remembered the way things were and longed for their old relationship the way she did.

"Gary, you know I don't want our marriage to be over. We've grown up together. You know me like nobody else. I just feel like you're not the same guy."

"I'm not the same guy," he said. Don't I have the right to be affected by my brother's death? How could that not change me?"

"I know loss changes people. Don't you think someone who used to be a nurse would realize that? That job did give me quite a bit of experience with death. I understand better than you know, but you have chosen to shut me out. I can't be there for you if you ignore me."

Gary had no more answers and no more comebacks. He conceded. She was right. He had been absent for his family, and it was causing him to miss out on anything and everything that could bring joy back into his life.

"This week, I've seen firsthand how hard it is to be solely responsible for the kids," he said. "I've put you in a tough position. I haven't been there for you since Mitch died."

Tears began rolling down Allison's face. Gary could hear her sobs. For the first time in a long time, she got to release her emotions. The tears were more from relief than anything else. She found tremendous relief in hearing Gary express he understood her situation. It showed her the old Gary had not been completely lost.

"Gary, I think we ought to get counseling. Why don't we go see Pastor Evans next week?" she suggested.

Without any hesitation or resistance Gary agreed to attend counseling with Allison. It would not be a quick fix to their problems. There was no such thing for problems so complex, but it was a step in the right direction.

"Allison," said Gary.

"Yeah Gary," she answered.

"I can't hang up this phone without telling you how much I love you. I've been missing you so bad since you left town. I'll be a better husband when you get home," he promised.

Gary had not told Allison he loved her in months. For the first time in a while, Allison went to bed happy. She felt a little of the spark that brought her and Gary together in the first place. If that spark was still there, the marriage could be salvaged.

Chapter 19

Monique left work a little early. She thought she would cook Bo's favorite meal. She felt so much guilt for her deceit. She hoped going to the trouble of making chicken fried steak with gravy, mashed potatoes and biscuits would grant her a feeling of atonement for her actions. To further atone, Monique was making Bo's mother's recipe for white cake with homemade caramel frosting. If it happened that Bo was to find out about the tape, nothing would say, "I've gone from sleazy stripper to Donna Reed" like a wholesome, homemade meal.

That evening, Monique sort of reminded herself of Donna Reed. She was still wearing her work clothes. The a-line cut, sleeveless black dress with a white trim around the bottom was something the television housewife might be wearing if the show would have been made in more recent years. Monique's glossy brown hair was pulled back into a French twist with a few pieces hanging loose around her face. To make herself more comfortable while cooking, she was barefoot and wearing a multi-colored polka dotted apron that looked like a bag of Wonder Bread.

Right about the time she expected him to pull into the driveway, the phone rang. Caller ID displayed Bo's cell phone number.

You've got to be kidding me, was Monique's first thought.

She was still learning to accept no matter how much effort was put into a dinner, a farmer's wife could never count on her husband making it home by suppertime. Monique ate many dinners by herself since marrying Bo. And lots of meals had been reheated in their microwave.

Bo did make an effort to try and be home by six thirty every evening, but cows and crops had minds of their own. Fences had to be fixed, sheep needed to be sheared and precautions had to be taken in threats of bad weather.

That night, of all nights, Monique was hoping Bo would be home early. She worked so hard on a special dinner and even harder on the script in her head of how their conversation about the tape would transpire.

As expected, Bo told her he would be late getting in from the farm. "Honey, I'm so sorry, but a tree fell and knocked out a whole section of fence. If I don't get it fixed, my cows will start getting out into the road," he explained.

Monique knew it would not be fair to express her aggravation. It was part of his job, and she knew Bo would never have normal hours when she married him.

"I know you can't help it," she said. Just come home as soon as you can. I've made country-fried steak, mashed potatoes and biscuits. I even made your favorite caramel cake."

Bo felt terrible about all the trouble his wife had gone to in making a meal that was sitting on the counter getting cold. "The thought of all that good food is going to make me work faster so I can get home to you and that supper!" he exclaimed.

After she got off the phone with Bo, Monique ate her dinner alone in front of the television. Before putting the food away, she made Bo a plate and wrapped it in plastic wrap.

All of the worry and deceit made her extremely tired. She laid down on the couch after she had cleaned up the kitchen. By the time Bo got home, the eleven o'clock news was coming on and she had fallen asleep on the couch.

He woke her with a sweet kiss on the cheek. "Honey, I'm so sorry I couldn't get home earlier. I know you went to a lot of trouble to make that meal. My plate looks delicious."

"I also made a white cake with caramel frosting. Want me to cut a piece for your dessert?" she asked.

"No sweetie, I'll get it. You go on to bed," he coaxed.

Monique wished she had the energy to sit and talk with Bo while he ate his dinner, but she just could not do it. It took too much out of her to face Bo, knowing what she was keeping from him. Her secret was already pulling her away from him. If she continued to keep the secret, it could only mean bad things for their relationship.

Chapter 20

By their last full day of vacation, the ladies were used to sleeping late. Dorothy slept till nine. Ten minutes later, both Allison and Marlene joined her for coffee.

Marlene came up with a plan for their morning. "Why don't we have a little bit to eat right now and go for a walk on the beach. Then I'll make us a good breakfast when we get back."

After the women got back from their walk, they were ready to eat something hearty. Before they left for their beach walk, Marlene had assessed what was left in the fridge. As they walked, she planned what she could make when they got back to the condo.

With seven eggs, some bagged spinach, chopped ham, an avocado, a tomato, some cheddar and a splash of half and half, Marlene cooked up some savory omelets. There was still half a loaf of Dorothy's sourdough bread. Marlene cut the loaf into thick slices, dipped it in a mixture of two eggs, sugar, mashed banana, a few tablespoons of orange juice and the last drops from the half-and-half carton. After the bread slices soaked up the liquid, Marlene fried them up into golden pieces of French toast. Leftover melon, cantaloupe, strawberries, and pineapple were tossed together into a beautiful fruit salad.

In thirty minutes, Marlene put the whole breakfast together. While she cooked, Allison made another pot coffee. Dorothy set the table on their back deck so they could eat outside.

While she took a big forkful of French toast, Dorothy closed her eyes and said, "This is as good as it gets."

Allison was most impressed by Marlene's creativity and ingenuity. "I can't believe you took what scraps we had left from the week and put this together. You are a genius with food!" she exclaimed.

Marlene thought it might be a good time to clue Allison and Dorothy in on her new idea for Cutie Pies. Whenever she wanted to try something new, Marlene liked running it by Allison and Dorothy. She could count on them for honest, constructive opinions.

"You all want to hear what I'm going to start offering at Cutie Pies when we get back?"

They were excited to find out what Marlene was going to do. "I'm sure we'll love it, as long as we get to be your test subjects," Dorothy joked.

Marlene went on with telling them about her new idea. "Have you guys heard of hand pies?" she asked.

Allison and Dorothy both shook their heads.

Marlene went on to explain. "Hand pies are little portable pies. They're sort of like turnovers. I first read about them in a food magazine that talked about how they are really popular food truck faire in Portland, Oregon."

Allison thought she knew where Marlene was going with her idea. "Portable pies would be great for people who want to take them to the park across the street and have picnics," she said.

Dorothy was grabbing hold of the concept. "With the new park becoming such a popular place for picnics and you being across the street from the park, there's a big market for food that people can grab and take over there."

Marlene felt encouraged. Her friends understood the appeal of hand pies within seconds of her presenting them with the idea. If she could so easily sell the rest of the town on her new product, she would be on the forefront of something good in Coleman.

"I will do savory and sweet hand pies. Just about anything you can put into a sandwich, pizza or casserole can be made into a good savory hand pie. The sweet hand pies are really just the turnovers I've been doing all along. The crust will be the same as my basic pie crust, so they are not going to be all that hard to add to my menu. I'll probably be able to do it by adding just one more employee."

Marlene named some of the flavors of hand pies she would be offering. Dorothy and Allison thought the pies sounded delicious.

Marlene promised her friends a private tasting before she put them on the menu. "We have to plan a time soon for you guys to come in and try them. I can't put them out to the public until they're friend tested," she assured.

Allison made a prediction. "Marlene, you're going to have people lined up out your door. You'll be selling those little pies hand over fist."

Dorothy made a correction. "No, she'll be selling them hand PIE over fist!"

Chapter 21

Monique decided she had to tell Bo about the tape that she had buried in the yard. Her mind kept going back to images of her family's dog digging up stuff in the yard. Somehow the tape or something about it was bound to resurface. Whoever had gone to the trouble to send it was likely to have more dirt on Monique. Other things from her past were likely to pop up. Keeping Bo in the dark about the tape could only lead her into a vicious cycle of one lie leading to another.

If whoever sent the tape did not blow the lid off her secret, some nosy neighbor was bound to do it. Few neighborhood occurrences managed to sneak past Francine. Her eyes were always peeking out some window of her house to see what her neighbors were doing. If Francine had seen her going into the woods to bury the tape, Bo AND the whole community would know what Monique had done.

Since she thought he might take things better on a full stomach, Monique made another stab at making Bo a special dinner. This time it was a simpler, yet sure to please dinner.

Bo loved Monique's spaghetti. It was the only meal he liked to have three nights in a row. *If he finds out about all this mess and kicks me out of the house, at least he'll have something to eat for a few days*, Monique thought to herself as she filled the slow cooker with ground beef, tomato sauce, chopped onions and Italian spices.

She set the slow cooker dial for ten hours. That would be about the time she would be getting home from work and Bo should be coming in from the farm.

Ten hours was going to feel like an eternity. While her sauce simmered for that long, Monique's emotions were also going to be bubbling and simmering. Her stomach went from feeling full of butterflies to feeling like she swallowed a capsule of baking soda and vinegar that would explode at any minute.

When Monique's brother was a kid, he used to make vinegar and baking soda bombs in plastic drink bottles. Dominique would shake those bottles and watch the caps pop off the top. The cap popping off would be followed by a blast of bubbly, fuming foam. Monique felt like everything she ate or drank since receiving the tape turned into that same burning, bubbling liquid.

Monique felt bad enough to stay home and take a sick day, but things were too busy at work for her to do that. Besides, work might take her mind off things.

She owned a tanning salon called Monique's Parisian Tanning Boutique. She had become so proficient in the art of the spray tan that people came to her from other towns to get a natural looking golden glow. If aliens were to land in Coleman, they would likely think all earthling women were perfectly bronzed, because it seemed like the whole town went to Monique for tans. Prom season was so busy that Monique saw a need to expand her business. She knew it was the right time for growth. As the new interstate project progressed, more and more businesses would be coming in. She wanted to establish herself before someone else with more money had a chance to come in with a bigger and better tanning business. The new building would be large enough for her to gradually add other services. Monique hoped to someday own a full-fledged spa.

Marlene's husband Mark helped her find a larger building. She was gradually moving things from one building to another, hoping to have the move be as seamless as possible. Her plan was to be open at her new location the very next day after she moved everything from her old location. It was the season for shorts and sundresses. Monique could not afford to be out of operation during a time when everyone wanted to have a tan. Hopefully, there was so much to do she would not allow herself any spare time to get nervous about the talk she would later have with Bo.

Monique's first appointment for the day was at nine-thirty. She decided to go in at nine to get some things done before that appointment showed up. As if she had not had enough stress for the day already, Whitley Dawn was waiting in the parking lot when she got there.

Whitley Dawn would rather slap Monique in the face than tell her "Hello," so Monique had to worry when she saw her car. In the thought that Bo would someday be her husband, Whitley Dawn went so far as to try and steal Bo away from Monique a mere few weeks before their wedding. Whitley Dawn's mission to steal Bo took an embarrassing turn.

After Bo and Monique's engagement, Whitley Dawn stopped eating, which led to a quick weight loss. With the help and encouragement of some Hens, she got a new hairstyle and bought new clothes.

In a last ditch attempt to snatch Bo away from Monique, Whitley Dawn unveiled her new look at a church fish fry where she knew both Bo and Monique would be in attendance. Whitley Dawn's Makeover caused quite a ruckus but was soon overshadowed by an unfortunate incident.

After accidentally plopping herself down on a blob of ketchup, Whitley Dawn excused herself from the fish fry. She went to an upstairs bathroom to clean the ketchup off her new jeans. So that Whitley Dawn could see a view of her backside before going back into the fish fry, she climbed up on the toilet lid and turned her behind towards the mirror over the vanity. In a humiliating twist of events, the toilet broke loose from the wall. What followed was an extremely embarrassing and difficult-to-explain scene.

The whole crowd at the fish fry ended up leaving the fish fry to see what was going on upstairs. A volunteer firefighter named Clyde Withers sensed danger lurked upstairs. He sprinted upstairs, making him the first person on the scene. Clyde busted through the bathroom door, flinging himself into Whitley Dawn, who fell and cracked her head against the sink. The crowd arrived upstairs to find Clyde and Whitley Dawn lying on the bathroom floor, soaked in water from the broken toilet.

A thoroughly humiliated and heart-broken Whitley Dawn became reclusive and gained back most of the weight she lost. The new hairstyle grew out and the stylish new wardrobe hung in the closet while Whitley Dawn pulled out her old nylon track suits or "swish-swish" suits as Monique liked to call them. The name "swish-swish" came from the noise the nylon pants made as Whitley Dawn walked.

Monique did not want to think Whitley Dawn was stalking her, but sometimes she could swear Whitley Dawn was turning up in odd times and at odd places. She would be out in the grocery store or walking around downtown and hear that tell-tale swish-swish coming from behind.

Monique would never put it past Whitley Dawn to be stalking her. The wedding of Bo and Monique did not keep Whitley Dawn from running her mouth. It got back to Monique that Whitley Dawn had predicted her marriage to fail within two years, plunging Bo back into Coleman's pool of eligibles.

Monique politely waved to Whitley Dawn and then went about unlocking the front door. She was hoping maybe Whitley Dawn was there to meet someone in the parking lot and would soon drive away. For good measure, she planned to lock the door behind her until her first appointment showed up.

Right as Monique was pulling the key out of the door, she heard a swish-swish coming towards her. "Hey Monique, can I talk with you a minute?" asked Whitley Dawn.

The hairs on the back of Monique's neck stood up when she heard Whitley Dawn behind her. All of the sudden, Whitley Dawn seemed a likely suspect behind the mysterious tape. The question was, if she was half as crazy as Monique thought she might be, why was she there and what was she about to do?

Chapter 22

The ladies never planned on running into anyone they knew during their Hilton Head vacation. They were completely bowled over when they ran into Glen Davis and Corrine DelRay-Cantrell-Robinson.

Running into Glen really should not have been such a surprise. He was like a recurring plantar wart to Marlene. Glen was an annoyance who kept popping up. It would not have surprised any of them if Glen came down to Hilton Head because he heard they were vacationing.

For about twenty years, he chased Marlene with tremendous perseverance. Every Friday, he would stop by Cutie Pies to buy a pie and ask her out. And every Friday she would turn him down as she handed him his boxed pie.

Once Marlene got married, Glen kept coming to Cutie Pies every Friday afternoon but directed his flirtations toward the Patton twins. Even Glen was bright enough to figure trying to get Emily or Anna to fall for a guy twice their age with half their morals was like trying to meet a ten dollar hooker at a Baptist tent revival.

Within minutes of getting word Charity was divorcing, Glen set his sights on her. Like a hound on the scent of a raccoon, when Glen found out a woman was getting a divorce, he was hot on her trail.

Glen was not completely without a few redeeming qualities. He was a great customer due to the fact he bought an entire pie nearly every Friday of his life without fail. He also proved most people had underestimated his work ethic. For a very long time, everyone saw Glen as being spoiled, lazy and entitled.

Right after high school graduation, Glen slid into a cushy, high-paying job for his parents' company. Glen's parents had a business that did fencing for yards, businesses and farms. They had worked tirelessly to make the business successful.

When they put Glen to work, his job description was short and his salary was sizeable. His parents' intentions were to have Glen do a variety of small tasks so he could understand every operation of the company. Their plan was to ease him into bigger responsibilities.

It took a while for Glen's work ethic to fully develop. He was not the least bit concerned with learning his parents' business. Glen fell pitifully short of earning the salary they were paying. Finally, his parents got tired of his freeloading. They gave him an ultimatum of either stepping up or stepping out of the business.

He then decided to strike out on his own. It was not because he was mad at his parents but rather because he really wanted to prove he was his own man. Glen thought about a business idea for some time and decided the moment was ripe to give it a go.

He began by contacting all his farmer friends. When several were on board, he launched Farm Fresh Goods. He began by selling beef delivered fresh from local farms. Once the beef proved profitable, Glen began delivering other agricultural products like milk, eggs and vegetables. He made himself the Schwan's of Coleman. He had three trucks that constantly ran the roads to nearly every business and at least half of the households in town.

Running a successful business proved Glen did have a little more going on under his baseball hat than people ever would have thought. He did have some brains and developed a work ethic. In some ways, Glen matured, except in the way he approached women.

Marlene spotted Glen first. It actually went though her head they might could get by him without being seen. They were walking across the dock of the Salty Dog Marina while Glen and Corrine were having drinks at a small table by the water.

Glen put highlights in his hair to disguise the gray that was beginning to show. The highlights, plus a tan that was way too dark and a big gold rope chain around his neck made him look like a male gigolo.

Not one to ever miss ogling a pretty lady, Glen noticed the three of them right away. "Well, my goodness," he said. "Ya'll come over here and love up on Glen a little bit."

They knew better than to "love up" on Glen. A simple hug or handshake never failed to become an unwanted sexual advance. Last time Allison got close enough for Glen to hug her, he put his hand in the small of her back within an inch of her buttocks and said, "If my hands slips a little onto that fine little bottom, you gonna slap me?"

Most women would not want their companion to be so flirty with another woman, but Corrine was too stupid to care. She was one of the most beautiful women to ever come out of Coleman. Sadly, she did not have the brains to match. The only thing Corrine was ever able to figure out was she had better latch onto a rich man. Lord knows she could not have taken care of herself.

The first millionaire she landed was Bruce Wilson. He was the richest guy in Coleman. Bruce broke off the engagement when he found out Corrine cheated on him.

After the broken engagement, Corrine and her mom moved to Myrtle Beach, South Carolina, where they met a couple of wealthy old men who owned some seafood restaurants. Corrine's old man passed away about five years after they got married.

Before long, she met a developer who built condos in Hilton Head. Corrine and husband number two divorced after only a year, leaving her free to pursue a new target.

After going through two rich husbands, Corrine found herself in a new situation. She was rich, so she no longer had to seek marriages to wealthy men. Glen and his family had plenty of money, but they were not in the super-rich elite with whom Corrine had previously mingled and married.

At the age of fifty-one, Corrine had become a bit of a cougar, preying on a man who was a few years her junior. Corrine and Glen knew each other from when she lived in Coleman. They had recently become reacquainted on Facebook.

Glen spent a great deal of his free time prowling Facebook for available females. A status of single opened the door for Glen's standard Facebook pitch. He was more eloquent on his computer than he was with his spoken lines. After he discovered Corrine's status while perusing Facebook, Glen sent her a sweet message confessing she was his first big crush as a kid. Corrine was both flattered and interested. She messaged back, and their Facebook relationship was off to a good start.

After weeks of communicating over the phone and computer, Glen made the trip down to Hilton Head. Glen and Corrine looked like there was some major physical chemistry between them. Even as Glen flirted with Marlene, Allison and Dorothy, he and Corrine were hanging all over each other.

They all hung out and talked for a short time before Glen's restaurant pager buzzed. "Oh, our table at the restaurant is ready," he said. "We've had the drinks out here. Now, we gotta get some food in us. Corrine and I are going to need some energy for what's in store tonight."

Marlene, Allison and Dorothy felt awkward standing there as Glen alluded to what he and Corrine would be doing later that evening. Sensing their discomfort and perhaps to protect her honor, Corrine explained Glen's statement. "It's not like it sounds," she explained. There's going to be a good band playing here later tonight. We're going dancing after dinner."

Glen showed he still had more than dancing on his mind. "Yeah, dancing and some other physical activities," he said.

Allison was sick of Glen to the point where she wanted them to go on their way. "Well, don't let us hold up your evening. Sounds like Glen has a full night planned," Allison said.

As Glen and Corrine walked away, Marlene laughed and rolled her eyes. "Of all the people we could run into when we're away from home. Thank God I let that one get away!" she said.

Soon after Glen and Corrine went in to eat dinner, the ladies were paged that their table was ready. They were seated close enough to see Glen and Corrine in the restaurant but not so close they had to keep talking to them. Allison had a hard time not watching the two. "We've got a bird's eye view right here of Glen and Corrine," she said. "I feel like a big perv watching them go at it, but I can't seem to turn away."

Dorothy turned to look. "We can stare at them this whole night, and they'll never notice. I feel like we're watching jungle cats mate on the Discovery Channel!" she said laughing.

Marlene resisted looking their way, but she had to see what Allison and Dorothy were talking about. "Wow, I feel like I'm a chaperone at a middle school dance catching two kids making out in the corner."

Glen and Corrine were eating and kissing, which seemed like a gross combination to Marlene. They would take a few bites of their dinners and then start kissing right at the table. Dorothy thought at the rate they're going, it will take those two three hours to eat dinner, with all of the make-out breaks they're taking.

Marlene, Allison and Dorothy ate their meals, paid their bill and were out the door of the restaurant long before Glena and Corrine.

After dinner, the ladies went to buy Salty Dog t-shirts for their families. Shopping for their kids made them all anxious to see them again. Marlene summed up a collective sentiment. "This vacation has been just what I needed, but I sure can't wait to see my little guy!"

Chapter 23

"Hey Monique, I hate to bug you early in the morning like this," said Whitley Dawn.

Monique kept her hand on the front door, ready to run inside and lock it behind her if Whitley Dawn said anything psychotic. She turned her head a little so she could look over her shoulder to see Whitley Dawn out of the corner of her eye. "It's okay. I'm just getting ready to open up. I've got an appointment coming any minute now," she lied.

In case Whitley Dawn had intentions of harming her, Monique thought it might be wise to let her know someone else would be showing up.

"Oh, I won't take much of your time. Do you have time to talk for a second?" asked Whitley Dawn.

Monique really did not have time to talk, but she was curious as to what Whitley Dawn had to say. "Sure, what do you need to talk about?" she asked.

Monique turned around, but she still kept on hand on the front door so she could quickly get inside and slam the door in Whitley Dawn's face if things got out of hand.

"I'm going to be in a wedding next month," said Whitley Dawn.

Monique's mind quickly filled in the next part of what Whitley Dawn would say. *The wedding is going to be mine and Bo's after he finds out about the tape that mysteriously wound up in your mailbox. Then he'll leave you and run to me.*

Whitley Dawn continued. "The bride has picked out these strapless dresses, and I'm white as a sheet. If I don't get a tan, I'll be the same color as the bride's dress. I've got to get a tan, and I hear you're the best person to do it."

Monique felt put on the spot. Was Whitley Dawn finding one more way to infiltrate her life? Would Whitley Dawn ask questions about her and Bo's relationship when she came into for tanning sessions?

There was the possibility Whitley Dawn was humbling herself by asking for Monique's help. Maybe there were no ulterior motives. Perhaps she did simply want a good tan. The rest of the Hens began coming to Monique for tans, and nothing bad had happened from her doing business with them.

The vengeful part of Monique could sabotage Whitley Dawn's tan. There were some hideous shades that could be created with spray tan chemicals. It was a tempting thought, but too unprofessional for a woman known for giving flawless, natural-looking results.

"Okay, come on in. We'll make you an appointment. Do you want to do your first tan right before the wedding, or do you want to give it a trial run so we can adjust the formula for your perfect shade?"

"I'd love to come in later today, if you have anything available. I've never had a spray tan, so I am excited to see what it will look like on me," said Whitley Dawn.

Monique made Whitley Dawn an appointment for that afternoon. She would get a beautiful spray tan. That is what Monique's Parisian Tanning Boutique guaranteed for their customers. Monique hoped she was not giving a boost in the looks department to a woman who was still after her husband by sending a mysterious videotape to her home.

Chapter 24

While the fact Glen was a big jerk was fairly obvious, Brad was coy about his bad intentions. He worked over many young girls. A naïve little Patton twin seemed like a piece of putty in his hands.

When Brad and Brent asked Emily and Anna for a date, they did not specify which girl was being asked out by which boy. The girls took it on themselves to decide which boy they wanted to date. It was decided that Emily would be with Brent while Anna chose Brad.

The match-up decision was made by Anna. Emily felt no particular attraction to either boy. She just thought they were both nice and cute. On the other hand, Anna thought Brad was the stuff her dreams were made of. As Erica and Rhonda were helping the twins get ready for their date, Anna told them Brad "knocks my socks off like boiled okra."

Rhonda and Erica were raised in the south, but Anna's saying was a new one for them. Emily explained what her sister meant. "Boiled okra is supposed to make your skin soft. Theoretically, if you eat enough of it, your skin could become so soft and silky that your socks would slip right off of your feet."

Emily did not show half as much enthusiasm about their date. "I'm excited because I think it will be fun, but I'm not expecting fireworks or anything. They're nice boys, but they live in another town. It would be hard to maintain a relationship with them off at college and us here."

Until that evening, Rhonda and Erica thought Emily and Anna were like two bookends; alike in every way. It was becoming clear Emily was practical, even cynical with her feet planted firmly on the ground. Anna was the twin with her head in the clouds, hoping for romance to come along.

Emily became concerned about her sister while they were getting ready for the date. "Anna, you seem like a different person. I don't understand your getting this way over a boy you hardly know."

"I knew the moment I that Brad first spoke to us at Carson-Newman that he's the one for me," said Anna.

"I sure hope you don't tell him that," replied Emily. "I might have to smack you or something. Such a premonition as he is your future husband isn't something you want to share on your first date."

Erica backed up Emily's advice. "Hard to get is what you want to be, especially on a first date."

* * *

Five minutes into their date, Emily could see her sister was not playing hard to get. They decided to have dinner in Langrid. Brent was driving, so he and Emily sat up front. Emily and Brent had the normal getting-to-know-you conversation. In the back seat, Anna was intent on listening to Brad talk non-stop about himself.

She smiled and giggled as he told her stories of his achievements and conquests. As Brad ran down his list of why he was such a good catch, his cell phone constantly alerted him to new text messages. Emily found it extremely rude that Brad took time to answer the test messages, even telling Anna some of them were from girls. Instead of angering Anna, or making her feel disrespected, she seemed to value Brad's attention more because she had to compete for it. "I feel like a lucky girl tonight,"she said. "All those girls get are texts while I'm having dinner with you."

Emily wanted to gag herself! A few minutes with a pompous boy had made her sister into a dizzy, spastic, silly mess of a girl.

Things did not get any better during dinner. Anna scooted her chair so close to Brad that she was practically on his lap, and Brad kept rubbing Anna's knee. At one point, she flirtatiously crossed her legs at the knee and rubbed Brad's ankle with her foot. Such displays of physical affection before marriage were discouraged in the Patton family. The girls were taught keeping physical affection to a minimum during courtship was the best way to avoid sexual temptation. Emily kept thinking her parents would die if they saw Anna and Brad acting so cozy on their first date.

Mr. and Mrs. Patton thought double dating was a safe-guard for their daughters, but Anna and Brad might as well have been alone. They were in their own little world while Emily and Brent had their date across the table.

Emily tried to ignore her sister and focus on enjoying her dinner with Brent. She was certain she wanted to out with Brent again. It was not that she felt any tremendous amount of chemistry with him. Brent was nice and all, but they seemed more suited as friends. Emily planned to keep going out with Brent because there was no way on God's Earth she would let her sister go out alone with Brad! If she could keep Brent interested, the double dates might continue. Otherwise, Emily was afraid that Anna and Brad would be going out alone.

Chapter 25

When Bo walked through the front door, a wave of panic undulated throughout Monique's body. It began at the top of her head and traveled quickly to the tips of her toes, winding its way through her stomach, leaving a path of searing panic throughout her body.

Bo walked into the kitchen and planted a big kiss on her lips. "Wow, dinner smells awesome. I'm in the mood for spaghetti. By the way, did a DVD come in the mail earlier this week?" he asked.

Monique had no way to cover her tracks anymore. "Yes, it came," she said.

"Oh, good! How about after dinner we watch that DVD?" Bo was so nonchalant Monique thought he could have been talking about something else, but he had to be referring to the tape she buried. It was the only movie that came in the mail.

Bo kept on talking about the tape as if it were no big deal. "I thought it would be nice to just relax tonight with a big bowl of popcorn and watch it," he said.

Was he making her squirm, or was he talking about something completely different? Regardless of Bo's awareness of the situation, Monique was sick of keeping a secret.

"So, what you are going to do? Make me watch it with you?" she asked.

Bo seemed stunned by the tone of her question. "Yeah, I think you'll enjoy it too," he said. I know it's probably more of a guy thing to watch. Some wives don't like to watch this silly, juvenile stuff with their husbands, but I thought you might want to see it. Myself, I'm curious what all the fuss is about."

Monique was getting strangely uncomfortable. Bo seemed excited about watching the tape. She would rather him be upset than turned on by it.

"I never thought you'd be into watching dirty movies with your wife," she said.

"Well, I don't think it's going to be all that dirty. I mean, I wouldn't show it to a little kid, but I doubt it's that bad. It sounds like it's almost a documentary made in West Virginia. I was even thinking about asking my dad if he wants to come over and watch it with us."

"A documentary? You might be talking about my life. What's on that tape could be humiliating to me. Are you just trying to make this as awkward as you possibly can? You really want me to watch it with your dad? Are you kidding? That's so sick!" she exclaimed.

"My dad was the first person to tell me about it," he said. "He's been kind of wanting to watch it. It takes place in West Virginia, but I don't think you should be so offended. It's not like the movie makes fun of everybody in West Virginia."

Monique then knew that there was a disconnect between what she was thinking and what Bo was a talking about. "Okay, you've lost me. What video are you talking about?" she asked.

"I told you, I ordered a video on Jesco White off eBay. Didn't I tell you about it? I bid $5 and won it. It's probably a bootleg copy for that price, but I thought I'd give it a try."

Monique felt like someone had just turned a switch that decompressed all of the pressure inside her head. When she realized how foolishly rash her behavior was, Monique did not know whether to burst out laughing or sobbing.

Their eBay account was set up in her name and registered to her credit card. So everything that she or Bo ordered off the site was addressed to her. Bo kept hearing things about the infamous "Dancing Outlaw," Jesco White of West Virginia. He had ordered a DVD about Jesco off eBay.

"Honey, why are you upset?" he asked. Bo was completely at a loss as to why his wife was being so weird about things.

"Bo, we need to take a walk," she said.

The confusion on Bo's face was growing more intense.

"Why honey, is something a matter?" he asked.

"Bo, let's get your shovel and take a walk out to the woods. This is going to take some explaining," she said.

As they walked to the spot in the woods marked by the rock where the tape was buried, Monique rehashed all of the events from the past week. By the time they started digging, both of them were laughing. Bo had to point out the absurdity of the moment. "I've never had to dig up a video before I watched it."

Right when they thought things could not get any more ironic, they noticed Francine was watching them. She was out in the corner of her yard, looking right at them as she watered her garden.

Feeling a little evil, Monique threw up her hand. "Hey Francine," she yelled.

Francine held up her hand, looking embarrassed, then quickly looked away. Bo was laughing harder after that. "Monique, you love to see those Hens squirm, don't you?" he asked.

"Yes, I do," she answered.

Since she knew the origin of the videotape, there was one Hen Monique was not as intent on making squirm. Knowing Whitley Dawn was not concocting a sinister plan to reveal her past via a mysterious tape was going to make it much easier to work with her. Whitley Dawn probably still had secret hopes of someday getting Bo, but Monique was once again assured that would never happen.

Chapter 26

"The Sand Tarts need to take one last walk on the beach before they go home," Dorothy said. Her friends thought it was a grand idea. Allison felt it was the perfect ending to their vacation.

It seemed like they might have run out of things to talk about after spending a whole week together, but they were just as chatty during that walk on the beach as they had been for the entire vacation. Mostly, they talked of their plans for when they got home.

They were both sad and excited to be leaving the beach. The rest and time they had with each other was both needed and deserved. While getting back to work and the daily grind was not going to be fun, they were all anxious to see their families. Surprisingly, Allison was as anxious to see Gary as Marlene and Dorothy were to see their husbands. "I think this may be the start of things turning around for us," she said.

After their walk, they all showered and packed their belongings. They were in the car and ready to roll by eleven that morning.

On the way home, Marlene called Charity to see how things were going at Cutie Pies. Charity would be leaving things in the hands of Adam, Emily and Anna for the day so that she could go to West Virginia. In exchange for running things while she was gone, Marlene was giving Charity a few days off so she could spend extra time in West Virginia for an extended weekend with her parents.

"Marlene, things went just great," said Charity. "We missed you, but we managed to keep things running smoothly. I went in early this morning to help fill all of our orders, so Adam and the Patton girls ought to be fine."

Once business had been discussed, Marlene asked about the recent developments in Charity's social life. "So, have you responded to Rick's offer for coffee?" she asked.

"Yes, I'm going to meet him. It's making me a nervous wreck," admitted Charity.

Marlene was surprised Charity was so worked up over having coffee with an old friend. She was normally so cool and calm about things. "Are you a good kind of nervous or a bad kind of nervous?" asked Marlene.

"I guess I'm sort of both. Back in high school, I used to get butterflies in my stomach when I was around Rick. Those butterflies are back. That's a good kind of nervous. At the same time, I feel guilty-as-can-be for making plans with another guy when Clay is so good to me," Charity admitted.

Allison and Dorothy were obviously listening to Marlene and Charity's conversation. They were beginning to whisper questions for Marlene to ask Charity.

"Charity, can I just put you on speaker phone? Allison and Dorothy are only hearing enough of this to drive themselves crazy. Dorothy practically has her ear against my phone trying to hear what you're saying."

"Go ahead and speaker phone me," answered Charity. "It will keep me from having to repeat my story."

"Okay, you're on speaker now."

"Alright, Allison and Dorothy. Let me catch you up. I had lunch with Charlotte. She always is a good person to discuss these things with. After talking to her, I decided I will have coffee with Rick, and I'm not going to tell Clay. Oh, and Charlotte surmised he may be a little too much like Joe."

Allison wondered what that meant. "How is Rick like Joe?" she asked.

"Well, I had not really thought about them being alike until Charlotte forced me to confront their similarities," said Charity. "My dad had the same feelings about Rick and Joe when he first met them. In high school, my parents would have never let me date Rick. They thought he was too wild and too cocky. Dad called him "Slick Rick," and he did not mean it as a compliment. Of course, with Joe I was an adult. Dad said the same things about Joe, but he couldn't keep me from dating him."

Dorothy wondered if the similarities might be making Charity nervous. "Are you apprehensive about meeting Rick now that Charlotte has pointed out that he sounds like another Joe?" she asked.

Charity knew she should be wary of Rick, but she was more excited than anything. "I suppose I should be running the other way, but don't worry. I learned my lesson. Trying to tame a bad boy almost did me in. I won't fall for this guy."

Marlene was already worried Charity was going to fall for the wrong guy again. "Charity, I know how you love bad boys. You sure you're not going to fall for this guy?" Marlene asked.

"I think I've learned my lesson from Joe. If Rick hasn't changed, he's history. It's just coffee, remember? We're not even going on a real date," she reminded.

Charity said one thing, but in her mind feared another. Could Slick Rick fool her into thinking he had grown up and was a nice, dependable guy when maybe he really was not? Was her dad right?

If Rick was a devil in disguise, could he pull one over on her?

One request was made by Charity before she hung up. "Be sure not to say anything if you guys don't mind. I don't want it to get back to Clay. I ought to be the one to tell him if he's going to find out. Also, I don't want Monique or Bo to find out about this, since Bo and Clay are cousins."

The ladies agreed to keep it all a secret. Charity's mention of Monique and Bo made Marlene change the subject. "Anybody talk to them this week. Wonder how they're doing."

* * *

Monique and Bo were doing just fine. Bo was not mad that his wife had kept her secret. "Honey, there's nothing from your past that could change how I feel about you," he said.

It was important to Monique that she explained to Bo that she had decided that she was going to tell him about the tape. "I couldn't stand keeping something from you. It was killing me," she said.

"Monique, I hate that you put yourself through all that. No more secrets, okay?" he asked.

If that week had taught her anything, it had taught Monique that keeping secrets takes too much energy. "No more secrets!"

Chapter 27

The Sand Tarts got back to Coleman around eight that evening. After Allison dropped Dorothy and Marlene off at their houses, she hurried home in hopes she would get there before Cicilly and Garret went to bed.

When she walked in the door, the kids met her with hugs and kisses. Allison could see her kids must have missed her as much as she missed them. While her kids were happy to see her, they did not act relieved as if she had rescued them from a week of misery. Cicilly and Garret both looked like they had been fed, rested and taken care of while she was gone.

"Where's your dad?" Allison asked.

Allison felt silly asking that question. She knew there was a ninety-nine percent chance he was down in the basement.

Cicilly said, "Mom, he's downstairs, but he's done really great this week."

Garret was also reassuring. "Dad's actually been pretty amazing. I think we're getting him back."

Allison had to see for herself. "Oh, kids I hope things are going to get better. I'm going to go down and see him," she said.

For the first time in a long time, Allison was anxious to get to the basement. It was the part of their house she had been calling "the gloom and doom room." The closer she got to the basement, the more Allison heard a strange popping noise. And there was an unmistakable aroma. The smell of popcorn was coming from the basement.

When Allison left her home to go to the beach, there was no way to make popcorn in her basement. Had Gary gotten a microwave for the basement? Sometimes, the only reason he ever left that room was to come upstairs to get some dinner. If Gary had a way to heat up Hot Pockets, the rest of the family might never see him again.

Allison found a pleasant surprise when she got downstairs. Gary bought an old-fashioned kettle popcorn popper for the basement. An even bigger surprise was Gary greeting her with a big kiss and warm embrace. When he said, "Allison, I've missed you so much," she believed him.

"Okay Gary. What's with the popcorn machine?" she asked.

"The kids and I thought we needed something down here to make it a better hang-out for all of us," he said. "I'm sick of being down here by myself all the time. I thought it would be fun to watch movies and have popcorn. I'm going to get a dorm fridge so we can have soft drinks."

Cicilly and Garret came down to see Allison's reaction. Garret had another surprise to show his mom. "Hey Mom, come out to the patio. We've got something else out there to show you."

Out on the patio was a brand new fire pit. Allison mentioned wanting to get a fire pit several months ago, but thought Gary ignored her request. "Gary, you remembered me saying I wanted one! I didn't even know you were paying attention when I said I wanted a fire pit."

Gary explained it was an early Mother's Day present. "The kids and I wanted to do something for you while you were gone. Do you like it?" he asked.

"Are you kidding? I love it!" she exclaimed.

Most of all, Allison loved what the fire pit and the popcorn popper symbolized. Popcorn and fire pits symbolized fun family time. Gary's surprises showed Allison he was ready to have some fun again and to spend time with his family.

Gary told Allison and the kids an idea he had for the evening. "How about I get the fire pit started so we can sit out here and roast some marshmallows?" she asked.

Garret went to find some sticks for the marshmallows, and Cicilly went to the kitchen for the bag of marshmallows, leaving Allison and Gary alone on the patio.

Gary walked over to Allison and grabbed her hand. "You surprised?" he asked.

Was she ever! "Gary, this is the best surprise of my life. I feel like you're back."

Allison was almost scared to get her hopes up. She knew Gary would continue to have some really difficult days ahead. "Gary, promise me something. I know you'll never get over losing Mitch. Just promise that when things get bad, you won't shut out me and the kids," she requested.

"I promise," he said. "I'll never do that to my family again."

Chapter 28

Charity was not one to fuss and primp, but she did put a little more effort than usual into getting ready for coffee with Rick. She chose to wear cropped jeans, a lavender crochet top and a pair of silver ballet flats. Charity put on a bit more make-up than usual and flat-ironed her blond hair until it was glossy and poker straight.

Charity's parents were keeping Blaney while she met Rick. She tried to convince them it was no big deal, but her looking so cute made them worry. Her dad expressed his concern. "You look awfully nice for this not to be a date. I sure hope this guy has changed if you're going to get involved with him."

"Dad, you worry too much," said Charity. "Meeting for coffee doesn't qualify as getting involved."

"I know how you fall for those bad boys. It just worries me for you and for Blaney. Whoever is in your life is in her life too," he said.

"Dad, I know that. That's why I refuse to get into a relationship right now. Blaney's my focus. A love life has to take a back seat to her."

* * *

When Charity walked into the coffee shop, she looked around but did not see Rick anywhere. She decided to order her coffee and take a seat. If she bought her coffee before Rick arrived, it was even less of a date. Going Dutch cancelled out any chance Rick could see their meeting as anything more than it was.

She had to wait more than ten minutes by herself. Charity was beginning to wonder if he stood her up. While she was waiting on Rick, Ashley Jones came in to get coffee.

Ashley went to school with Charity and Rick. She was one of the most beautiful girls in town. Rick dated her for about two years when they were in high school. Their relationship was constantly troubled because Rick was such a ladies' man. Ashley tried hard to hold Rick's attention, but his constant flirting and rumored cheating finally broke them up.

Ashley and Charity always had a strained relationship because of the time she and Rick spent together. Charity once tried to explain to Ashley that she and Rick were truly nothing but friends. The insincerity from wishing Rick was more than her friend must have come through in Charity's voice, because Ashley would not buy it.

Charity was hoping Ashley would not see her, but she did. "Hi Charity, what are you in town for?" asked. Ashley.

"My little girl and I are visiting my parents this weekend," Charity replied.

"Oh, Rick said you have a little girl," said Ashley. "Yeah, he mentioned something about you coming in this weekend to see your family."

Obviously, Ashley spoke to Rick and wanted Charity to know. If Ashley was being catty, Charity was going to return the cattiness.

"Rick actually is meeting me here for coffee," Charity said.

Ashley looked sort of irked. "Oh, well tell him I send my regards."

The words were not unkind, but the tone was icy and sharp, like a cold shot of strong tequila. It made Charity wonder why Ashley and Rick had been talking.

Charity was about to leave and forget she ever made plans with Rick. Then Rick walked in. He was better-looking than in high school. Rick was taller, broader through the shoulders and strutted with even more confidence.

When he sat down, he gave that smile that always made Charity feel fluttery. Rick had a smile that made him look a little mischievous. His incisors were so pointed Rick resembled a cartoon bat when he smiled. Her dad thought it made Rick look evil and cunning, Charity found it endearing.

She tried hard to avoid eye contact with Rick. His eyes fascinated her. They were such a deep brown that they were almost black. Looking into them gave Charity the same feeling of jumping into a lake at night. It was cool but eerie at the same time, because no one could ever know what was under the surface. Rick was dangerous and mysterious in that way.

They sat and talked for two hours. Charity planned to ask Rick why he was so late and how Ashley knew she had a kid, buts she did not get to either question. Those concerns vanished along with her resolve not to fall for him. Anyway, Charity was sure there were simple explanations. She may have misunderstood the time Rick said for them to meet. Rick probably ran into Ashley recently. The town was small. They were bound to cross paths from time-to-time. Charity felt no need to ask any questions or to worry about future implications getting involved with Rick might entail. Once again, the devil in disguise had worked his magic.

Chapter 29

Gary was doing so much better since Allison got back from Hilton Head. His grief was not, nor never would be erased, but it was managed. Gary began spending time with the family again and even seemed to be enjoying his life. He was still doing the "Love, Mitch" care packages but had scaled back a bit on the project to make more time for Allison and his kids.

In an effort to try and keep the good energy going in her home, Allison decided to throw a cookout to kick-off Memorial Day weekend. The party was going to be simple with hot dogs, hamburgers, a few friends and family. It was nothing elaborate, just enough to keep Gary's spirits up without overwhelming him.

With it being Memorial Day Weekend, the care packages for soldiers would be the focus. Everyone was to bring some items for the packages. After dinner, they would all work on assembling the care packages. At some time during the assembly, they would Skype with Mitch's widow Shelly so that she and their kids could see what everyone was doing.

The care packages would be delivered to the post office in a very special way. Charlotte's boyfriend, Chuck, was a member of the Patriot Guard. Chuck and some other Patriot Guard members were going to put flags on their motorcycles that had the "Love, Mitch" website printed on them. So far, Chuck had assembled about twenty Patriot Guard. The sight of all of those men on their bikes would draw some good attention to "Love, Mitch."

On the day of the party, the house was all abuzz so everything could be in place before Gary got home from work. While her kids strung up red, white and blue balloons all over the house, Allison was in her kitchen making food. The party was supposed to begin in an hour. Allison's mom and mother-in-law both came over to lend a hand.

Allison's mom was in charge of making the tea. She tried to adhere to Allison's system. "Regular sweet tea goes in the clear glass pitcher. Decaffeinated sweet tea goes in the plastic pitcher, and unsweetened decaf tea goes in the white ceramic pitcher. Is that right Allison?" she asked.

Allison looked up from the pan of sausage pinwheels she had just pulled out of the oven. "Yes mom, but don't worry about it. Nobody's going to die if they get a sip of the wrong kind of tea."

Quickly, Allison realized she said the wrong thing. Her parents knew at least one person who knew someone who died of any possible cause imagined. Her mom was quick to remind her their cousin Addie lived beside a woman whose aunt refrained from caffeine. "Addie's neighbor's aunt said it just made her heart race something awful if she had a cup of coffee. She said one time, she drank a bottle of Coca Cola, and it nearly made her heart beat out of her chest. Well, Addie's neighbor's aunt had a couple cups of coffee at a restaurant. Then her heart went to beating like crazy. She asked the waitress, 'Are you sure this is decaf?' That waitress looked at the pot she was carrying and realized that she had been pouring coffee with caffeine her cup. You see restaurants, use pots with two different colors of lids to know which pot is decaf and which is regular. That waitress was carrying the regular coffee pot and pouring it in Addie's neighbor's aunt's coffee cup. That woman died later in the night."

Allison heard the story of Cousin Addie's neighbor's aunt before. The aunt was ninety-two when she passed in her sleep.

Still, because she had two cups of coffee with caffeine that day with lunch, it was assumed by the family caffeine made her heart beat so hard it stopped. Not wanting to dispute such sound logic, Allison assured her mom she correctly matched iced tea to the proper pitchers.

On the other side of her kitchen, Allison's mother-in-law was frosting cupcakes. The repetitive action of dipping the knife in a bowl of fluffy butter cream frosting, then gliding it around each cupcake seemed to be putting her in a trancelike state. Allison often wondered what was going on inside her mother-in-law's mind. It was so perplexing to Allison how she could be so angry yet, at the same time, sympathetic towards Gary's mom. After all, they lady had lost a beloved son. As a mother, Allison could only imagine her pain from losing a son. Sometimes she wanted to shout, "You've still got a son, and you are killing him with your sadness! Your grandchildren love you, and you barely speak to them anymore."

She hoped Gary took the lead to march his family out of their seemingly endless pit. His recent gains toward becoming engaged in his life again might be something his parents would follow. Gary's strides towards normalcy could be turned backwards if his parents would not encourage him to move on with things.

Gary's dad came into the kitchen to see if his wife needed any help. "Want me to frost some cupcakes with you?" he asked.

Without saying a word, Gary's mom handed his dad a knife, and he began frosting in the same rhythmic trance as his wife. Allison had not had a proper conversation with her in-laws in months. She decided it might be the right time. Allison's mom just carried out tea pitchers, so she was alone with them.

"Hey guys, I appreciate you two coming over to help with this," she said casually.

They only looked at Allison and nodded their heads to acknowledge they heard her. Getting them to engage in conversation was going to take some work.

"Gary really seems to be doing better lately," she continued. "I was worried about whether or not we would get through this for a while. He shut me and the kids out. The kids and I missed him and finally feel like we're getting Gary back."

Allison was hesitant to begin her next sentence. "The kids miss their grandparents too."

Gary's mom's eyes filled with tears. "I know, we've got to snap out of it. This has been the hardest thing I could have ever imagined," she sobbed.

Gary's dad shared something with Allison. "We have decided to join a support group for parents of service men and women who have lost their lives in the line of duty. It meets once a month at the VA hospital in Johnson City. We're thinking it can help us deal with this thing," he said.

It was a big step and really all Allison could hope for. Gary's parents realized they needed to get help and had taken steps towards getting that help.

Allison commended them. "You two are so brave to reach out for help. I think you'll be glad for the support," she reassured.

Gary's mom reiterated what Elle told them back in Spartanburg. "We've missed out on so much with our grandkids since Mitch died. We need to start having some good times with them again."

Allison told them about something she and Gary discussed the night before. "We were talking about maybe trying to go back to Key West with you guys, Shelly and all the kids."

The first Christmas after Mitch died, the family went to Key West for the holidays. Gary thought it would be easier to get through their first Christmas without Mitch if they went on a trip instead of staying home for their traditional Christmas celebration.

"Gary thought it might be nice to do a summer vacation together this year," she said.

His parents seemed positive about the idea. Gary's dad said, "It can give us something to forward to. Mitch would have wanted us to keep going to the beach together. He loved family beach vacations."

Allison was so glad she talked with her in-laws. She was finally beginning to see the family was healing. Cicilly and Garret were getting back their father and their grandparents.

Chapter 30

Emily and Anna came by the party with Brent and Brad. Emily hoped Brad would show his true colors at the party so someone outside the family could tell Anna she was getting involved with the wrong kind of boy.

The brothers had been coming to Coleman every weekend to take Emily and Anna on a date. Emily still did not like Brad any better than she did the first time they all went out. It was excruciating to watch her sister fall in love with him, but Emily did not have the heart to say anything about it to Anna.

The only person she confided in was her father, who felt the same way about Brad. Together, Emily and her dad prayed about the situation. Emily was not one to tell God what to do, but she sure hoped the party provided an opportunity for others to see and confront the problem of Brad the Cad.

To Emily's dismay, Brad was the perfect party guest. He was witty, spoke to everyone and played with all of the children out in the yard. Brad knew how to ooze charm for a crowd. It was when there was not many people around that he showed his true personality.

Of all the people at the party that Brad could choose to buddy up with, he really clicked with Rick. *Slick Rick and Brad the Cad, how perfect*, thought Emily.

It was a surprise to everyone Charity brought Rick. Her move seemed to symbolize things were officially over between her and Clay. After Charity met Rick for coffee, she talked to Clay about cooling things off for a while.

As things were cooling off with Clay, Charity and Rick's relationship was heating up. They were seeing each other every couple of weeks. This new development in Charity's love life did not please her parents or friends.

Charity had introduced Rick to all of her buddies in Coleman. None were impressed, but most tried to be diplomatic in the way they communicated their feelings to Charity. Marlene delicately told Charity, "We don't really know Rick yet, but he doesn't seem to be as sweet as you."

Charlotte was the only one of Charity's friends who laid it all out. "Charity, I can't put my finger on it, but there is something about him that rubs me the wrong way. Actually, I can put my finger on it. From someone who knows, I can tell you I have to wonder if he has someone else back in West Virginia. All the signs are there. He doesn't call you when he says he will. He often won't answer the phone when you call or text him, and he's always at least an hour late when he's coming to see you. When Glen was cheating on me, he did all of those same things."

Charity reminded Charlotte that she also was the victim of a cheating man. "I know the signs," said Charity. "Remember, I've been through it myself? This isn't anything like my relationship with Joe. Besides, I don't even know if you could call this a relationship. We're just hanging out. It's no big deal. I haven't even introduced Rick to Blaney. If I was serious about him, don't you think I'd have him meet the most important person in my life?"

As much as Charity was trying to convince Charlotte she had not developed feelings for Rick, it was obvious she cared for him. If the relationship was not a big deal, Charity would not have put so much energy into arguing over it.

The devil in disguise had worked her over and was stressing her out. Charity was already defending him to her family, her friends and to herself. The only wise move she had made since meeting Rick for coffee was not introducing him to her daughter. Charity was extremely protective of Blaney. Problem was, she did not know how to protect her own heart from getting broken.

Chapter 31

One nice thing about all of their houses being so close together was Dorothy and Marlene could send their husbands and kids home early because they could walk back home whenever they wanted. After everyone left the party, Marlene and Dorothy stayed to help Allison clean up.

Once the house was picked up, Allison, Dorothy and Marlene hung out on the front porch with a pitcher of green apple martinis. Dorothy made an announcement. "Girls, I've got a surprise for each of you," she said.

Marlene wondered what it could be. "You're not going to make us guess are you?" she asked.

Allison, who still suffered with baby aches from time-to-time, hoped maybe another little one was coming into their lives. "You and Tom adopting again?" she asked.

"No, no. We're done," said Dorothy. "Darla's all we need. I gave Tom a bunch of our beach photos to make albums."

Tom was a very talented photographer who had a very artful way of composing photo albums.

Dorothy excused herself for a minute to go back in the house and grab a tote she carried in earlier. She came out with a stack of scrapbooks covered in an aquamarine shade of blue linen fabric. The cover of the book had a photo of the iconic lighthouse at

Harbour Town. The photos inside of the book chronicled their week together.

The last page of the book had two photos. At the top of the page was the photo Dorothy saved from Senior Week when they were eighteen. Below it was the picture Glen took of them in front of the Salty Dog Cafe.

Marlene thought they looked different in lots of ways but the same in others. "We've developed a lovely patina," she commented.

Allison was not following. "What the heck are you talking about? That sounds like some kind of painful rash or something."

"You know a patina, like furniture. Over the years, it collects layers of paint and age that develop into a finish that's beautiful. People try to fake a patina, but it never looks authentic. The only true way is through age and distress," she explained.

Dorothy liked what Marlene was saying. "Ah, that's awesome! The wrinkles around my eyes, the spider veins on my legs; it's all part of my patina. That sounds so much better than saying I'm getting older."

Allison liked it too. "Well said Marlene. I've sure earned my patina lately."

Below the photos of them on their last trip was the caption "Sand Tarts Forever!"

There was only one thing Marlene did not like about that last page of their scrapbooks. "These pictures were taken twenty-seven years apart. Let's promise we won't wait so long to do it again. Now that we're Sand Tarts, we've got to hang out at the beach more often.

Dorothy topped off all their glasses with what was left in the pitcher. She raised her glass to propose a toast "Sand Tarts Forever!"

Final Words from the Author

Cutie Pies Chronicles readers have kept the series going.
Thank you so much for wanting to read more of what I write.
Tammy, this series happened because you were willing to take
a risk with an eager, first time writer. Thank you for seeing me
through this process. Pam, thank you for making the covers of
my books so intriguing. The compliments on my covers never
stop! Sloane, I am so glad you are part of the MGP/LCB family.
Thank you for your diligent editing of my numerous faux pas!
Anna, thanks for helping me take my website from pitiful to
something I am proud for people to peruse. I want to thank
my friends and family for encouraging and supporting me in
everything I do. Last of all, I thank God for hearing the prayer
of a little girl who wanted to write a book someday.

A Taste of Cutie Pies

Hand pies are a great little treat. Enjoy these recipes that I came up with in my own kitchen. Unlike Marlene, I made use of some convenient time-savers from the grocery store that stand in for homemade pie crust.

Cheeseburger Hand Pies

These are so easy and so good! Sometimes I use the biscuits with flaky layers. Each biscuit can be separated into two or three thinner biscuits, so that the crust is not too thick. Take these to your next tailgate or potluck. They will disappear in minutes.

Brown a pound of ground beef. Once the beef has been browned, stir your favorite cheeseburger condiments into the cooked beef (ketchup, mustard, onion, pickle relish, etc.) Heat thoroughly.

Next, flatten a canned biscuit with the palm of your hand or rolling pin. Spoon some of the ground beef onto half of the flattened biscuit. Top the beef with shredded cheddar cheese. Fold the biscuit over to cover the beef and cheese. Seal egdes with tines of a fork. Continue until you have used all of your biscuits. Bake at 350 until biscuits are browned (about 15–20 minutes).

Apple Cinnamon Hand Pies

I came up with these as a breakfast treat for my daughters. They are good in the morning or for an afternoon coffee break.

Finely dice 1–2 apples. Flatten out a cinnamon roll with the palm of your hand or a rolling pin. The side of the cinnamon roll with all of the cinnamon bits on it should be facing up. Place 1–2 tablespoons of apple on half of cinnamon roll. Fold other half of cinnamon over apples. Seal edges of cinnamon roll with the tines of a fork. Continue with remaining apples and cinnamon rolls.

Bake at 350 for 15–20 minutes minutes. While hand pies are hot, frost top of hand pies with icing that is included with cinnamon rolls.

Chocolate Strawberry Hand Pies

Strawberries dipped in chocolate are one of my favorite desserts in the whole world. Using a can of crescent rounds, I created these little pies. If you cannot find crescent rounds, make triangular pies using regular crescent rolls.

Finely chop about 5 strawberrries. Flatten crescent round with the palm of your hand or a rolling pin. On half of crescent round place about 10 chocolate chips and 3–4 pieces of the chopped strawberries. Fold other half of crescent round over chocolate and strawberries. Seal edges with tines of fork. Continue until you have used all of your crescent rounds.

Bake at 375 degrees for 15 minutes.

Pizza Hand Pies

A pizza hand pie is a fun spin on a food that both kids and grown-ups love. You may used a pizza crust mix, pre-made pizza dough or your own recipe for crust.

Tear off small balls of pizza dough from your batch of prepared dough. Flatten dough with palm of your hand or rolling pin. Pizza dough tends to be sticky, so you may want to flour some waxed paper or parchment paper and flatten the dough on it. If perfect circles are important to you, use a glass or biscuit cutter to cut circles. I am okay with a more rustic look, which leads me to forgo cutting out circles.

Once the dough balls are flattened, spread your favorite pizza sauce on half the dough. Layer mozzerela cheese and desired pizza toppings (pepperoni, sausage, onions, green peppers, spinach, etc.) over the sauce.

Fold other half of dough over toppings. Seal edges with tines of fork. Make a tiny slit in top of hand pie so steam can escape.

If you want, you can brush tops of hand pies with olive oil and sprinkle with Italian herbs and/or parmesean cheese.

Bake at 425 degrees for 15–20 minutes. Serve with warmed pizza sauce for dipping.

About the Author

Lisa Hall writes from her home in Fall Branch, Tennessee. She is married to Todd and has two young daughters. In addition to the Cutie Pies Chronicles, Lisa has written a children's book that has been accepted for publication. She has several short stories included in published anthologies.

Lisa earned an undergraduate degree from Carson-Newman College and a Masters from East Tennessee State University. She spent ten years working for local school systems as a guidance counselor and assistant principal.

Lisa began her writing career after taking a parental leave from her job. A leave of absence that was originally intended to last one year has lasted for six years. In addition to writing, she does public speaking, writing workshops and teacher in-services.

The Cutie Pies Chronicles

Lisa Hall

Join the fun in Coleman, VA, where "Mayberry meets Desperate Housewives!" *The Cutie Pies Chronicles* is a clever series set in small town Virginia filled with the hijinks, gossip and relationships that shape the life of Marlene, the owner of the local bakery called Cutie Pies, and her two best friends, Dorothy and Allison!

Look for the fifth and final *Cutie Pies Chronicles* book titled, *Goodbye Cutie Pies*, coming in 2012!

Cutie Pies FOR Small Fries

Coming in 2012!

Burton the Sneezing Cow

Lisa Hall

A cow that is allergic to grass and hay might as well be lactose intolerant! B*urton the Sneezing Cow* tells of one cow's dilemma.

Allergies are making Burton one miserable cow! In desperation, he turns to Farmer Stanley for help. Burton knows he is in trouble when Farmer Stanley calls Dr. Brown. According to Hattie the Red Hen, Dr. Brown is a mean fellow. In a panic, Burton decides that the only thing to do is move into town. There his allergies will not be a problem.

In the end, Burton discovers that he should not have listened to Hattie the Red Hen. Just like the Hens cause problems in the Cutie Pies Chronicles, another type of Hen causes problems in *Burton the Sneezing Cow*!

For more information about the author, visit www.lisahallauthor.com!

Keep checking back at www.littlecreekbooks.com for more information!